The Mask That Sang

the mask that sang

SUSAN CURRIE

Second Story Press

Library and Archives Canada Cataloguing in Publication

Currie, Susan, 1967-, author
The mask that sang / by Susan Currie.

Issued in print and electronic formats.
ISBN 978-1-77260-013-1 (paperback).--ISBN 978-1-77260-014-8 (epub)

I. Title.

PS8555.U743M37 2016   jC813'.6   C2016-903531-X

C2016-903532-8

Cover by Gillian Newland

Editor: Kelly Jones
Designer: Melissa Kaita

Printed and bound in Canada

*Second Story Press gratefully acknowledges the support of the
Ontario Arts Council and the Canada Council for the Arts for our
publishing program. We acknowledge the financial support of the
Government of Canada through the Canada Book Fund.*

ONTARIO ARTS COUNCIL
CONSEIL DES ARTS DE L'ONTARIO
an Ontario government agency
un organisme du gouvernement de l'Ontario

Canada Council   Conseil des Arts
for the Arts   du Canada

Funded by the Government of Canada
Financé par le gouvernement du Canada | Canadä

Published by
SECOND STORY PRESS
20 Maud Street, Suite 401
Toronto, ON M5V 2M5
www.secondstorypress.ca

This book is for my daughter Rachel, whose insight and compassion humble me daily; it is also for my new birth aunt, Bev Hazzard, who handed me the gift of my own identity.

chapter one

Faster, faster! Cass kept scrambling past garbage cans and over cracked pavement, although her legs were dead stumps and her lungs screamed. The boys were close behind her, the same four who chased her every day.

"Hey! Food bank! Wait up!"

"Didn't your mother tell you it's rude to run away?"

Something whizzed past her ear and crashed into a parked car. Its alarm burst to life, fuzzy in her ears, already behind her.

Only another block, and she was home.

"Where'd you get those shoes? I want to get me a

pair like that!" Their laughter pierced like the skewers they wanted to stab her with.

Keep running!

But suddenly one of them was beside her, and another on the other side. Someone's foot hooked around her own, and she fell, hard. The knees on her pants ripped, and the skin underneath. But Cass refused to cry out.

"Just gonna lie there?"

Again came the laughter that meant to wound.

She got to her knees, not looking them in the eyes.

"You should stop when people are calling you, greasy hair."

Cass climbed slowly to her feet, facing them.

"Hey, what are you boys doing?"

Someone was leaning out of a car window, but his face was blurred because of the water in Cass's eyes.

"You leave that girl alone. What's wrong with you? Get out of here!"

"We're not doing anything."

"I watched, you knocked her down. Now you get lost, the four of you. Pack of bullies!"

The car door opened as Cass swiped the weak moisture away. She stood like a dead tree as the boys scattered in the face of someone stronger than themselves.

"You okay, sweetheart?"

She nodded dumbly.

"You should tell your teacher, tell your daddy about that. Tell an adult."

Cass nodded again. She would get right on telling her daddy. Just as soon as she knew who he was.

"Seriously. You gonna be all right? How old are you? You live near here?"

"I'm twelve. I live—just up the street."

The man scratched his head. He was torn, Cass could tell, between helping and getting on his way.

"Well, I gotta go. I'm late for work. Do you want me to walk you home?"

She shook her head. From her dry throat, she croaked, "Thanks."

"No problem, sweetheart. Seriously, tell your daddy. He'll put a stop to those jerks."

Then he was in his car, good deed done, off and away to his own life.

Cass jiggled the key in the lock. There was a trick to it, but she hadn't mastered it yet. When they'd lived here longer, it would be easy—that's what Mom had said, smiling brightly with an arm around Cass. But Cass doubted they'd be here long enough to learn the trick. Mom's new job cooking at the motel restaurant didn't

3

sound any more promising than the last one.

At last the key turned, and she fell into their studio apartment, a little room that had a bed in the corner, a kitchen on the other side, two chairs and a table.

Cass sank into one of the chairs and hugged herself. Tried to make it all go away.

One day, one day, she and Mom wouldn't live here. One day, they'd find the place that Cass imagined in her mind. It was a place of green trees, calm lakes. There weren't any bullies there. When Cass closed her eyes and breathed slowly, sometimes she could make that place appear before her. It made her feel almost homesick, although she had never lived anywhere like that.

She shut her eyes now and tried to make it appear.

There was just the rushing of faraway water at first, but the water came nearer and with it the breeze that whispered of green spaces, air to breathe.

And then Cass imagined that she could rise up on that singing wind. She was floating, soaring, high above the world. Below, the granite city was gone, replaced by a great blue-green lake that stretched out.

Cass directed the wind to lower her till it placed her gently on the water. The water moved her up and down. There was no place for bullies here, or fear—only sweet, undulating water.

ↃⱭ

Mom was fiddling with the key in the lock.

Cass scrambled up. Shadows had seeped across the room, all that was left of the lake and the music. What time was it, anyway?

"My sweetheart!"

Mom burst into the room, all paper bags and smiles and arms outstretched. Banishing everything bad, instantly filling the space with her own sunshine.

"How is my darling?" She swung the bags on the table and shrugged off the thin coat, dropping it on one of the chairs. She turned and cupped Cass's face in her hands, with eyes that saw her and loved her and worried. "Okay today? Not too bad? Not too scary?"

"No," Cass lied. "Not too bad."

Mom kept looking in her face. "Hmm."

"Just some boys, they were laughing at my shoes and stuff."

Mom hugged her, hard. And she didn't say anything, because there really wasn't anything more to say. Mom had even gone in to see the principal, one of the scariest things she'd ever done, Cass knew, because Mom was just about as afraid of everything official as Cass was.

The principal had promised to fix the problem. And it was better, when teachers were around. Trouble was, they couldn't walk her home.

"You are going to have gorgeous shoes one day," Mom said. "And they are going to be made of—what's good?"

"Leather," said Cass. She thought of books she'd read. "Or—or kid. Like a baby goat, not a, you know, *kid*."

"Kid," said Mom. "With sequins and lights that blink when you walk, and inserts that make you feel like you're walking on air. And they'll play your favorite song when you jump up and down, and bluebirds will come and sit on them and sing along."

When Mom talked like this, Cass couldn't help but get caught up in it. "And glow-in-the-dark shoelaces."

"Duh." Mom started to unpack the food bank bags. "Glow-in-the-dark shoelaces that transport you through time and space. Because, you see, we're going to discover that we are the only living heirs to royalty, and everyone who's royal wears these shoes. It's kind of your ticket into the club."

She placed tins of spaghetti on the table. "Tonight, I think, pasta à la Mommy?"

"Aren't you home early?"

"Yep, a little bit!" The cheerfulness in Mom's voice was suddenly forced. She had her face inside the large brown bag, getting the stuff at the bottom.

"Mom," said Cass softly. And she felt like the mom herself.

Her mom let out a big breath. "Oh, honey."

"Did something happen?"

"Yes," said Mom. "It did. I'm sorry, sweetheart. I saw the boss yelling at the new little girl for something she didn't do, and he had her backed right up against a wall, right in her face, making her cry."

Cass waited.

Mom sat down. "I got involved, and he fired me."

For a minute she wilted, the sunshine cut off. And for that minute you could see right inside, past the smiles and bright words, to the scared Mom beneath, who never seemed to get a break. Who wrecked the break when she got it, by telling the boss to stop bullying.

You couldn't beat a bully. Not at school, not at work, Cass thought.

Then Mom smiled. "So. I know what I'm doing tomorrow. Pounding the pavement. Don't worry, I'll get something else. There's lots around, lots of places willing to pay under the table. I'll have something by the time you get home tomorrow, I promise."

She cupped Cass's chin in her hands again.

"Don't worry, my baby."

☙

Bzzz! The doorbell sounded. They both jumped.

"Who could that be?"

"Maybe your boss wants to apologize," Cass said.

Mom smoothed her clothes with shaking fingers and ran a hand over her hair. "It's dark. We don't know anyone here."

She fumbled with the door, then put the chain on and opened it a fraction. "Yes?"

"I'm looking for Denise Jane Foster." The voice was a man's, very official sounding.

"That's me." Mom stood a little straighter.

"Twenty-seven years old, born July seven?"

"Yes. Did I do something wrong?"

"This is for you," said the man's voice. A large envelope passed through the door.

"Thank you." Mom looked at it anxiously. "Is it—is it a legal thing?"

The voice wasn't unkind. "I can't comment on that, just the messenger. Have a good night."

The man's steps receded down the hall.

Mom closed the door and locked it again. She stared down at the envelope.

"Well, open it!" Cass said.

"I don't know what it could be." Mom fingered the envelope nervously. At last she ripped it open, and slid out a pile of papers. Her eyes darted back and forth across the pages, wide and worried.

And then her face turned a strange color of putty, and she collapsed right down onto the floor.

chapter two

It was horrible after that. Mom was all shaky and dialing a number, while Cass hugged her knees amid the pillows on the bed. Dinner was forgotten, but Cass didn't care. Her stomach had gone tight, and she couldn't eat anything anyway.

Mom was saying, "I don't understand how you even found me. My mother abandoned me as a baby, she gave me up to Children's Aid and never tried to find me. I've been in over twenty foster homes, and I've lived at about as many addresses since. There is no way you have the right person."

Later: "Well, if she wanted to meet me so much, she

should have made an effort over the last twenty-seven years. I was around the whole time."

Cass hugged herself tighter, hearing the harsh words coming out of Mom's mouth. She never wanted Mom to talk to her like that.

"I'm not sure I'm interested in coming to your office," Mom's cold new voice said. "To be honest, it would cost money to get there, and that's money I don't have, as I'm in between jobs. No, I don't have a car."

More talking at the other end.

"Well, I'm not agreeing to anything if I do come. Just a meeting, that's all. And I can tell you in advance I don't plan to accept anything from her."

In the end, when everyone was finished talking, Mom hung up. Then she stared at her hands as they quivered. Cass looked at her own. They were doing the same.

"Mommy," said Cass, and ran to her, nearly bursting into tears. "What's wrong?"

"Nothing, my darling." It was Mom's warm voice again, thank goodness. "Just a lawyer, and just a thing. I have to go into the city tomorrow to see her, and she's sending a car to pick me up. That's all. No big deal."

But it was a big deal, Cass could tell. And Mom was so shaken by it Cass couldn't imagine her going by herself. Mom was a mess when it came to people she thought were important. She didn't think she counted in comparison.

"Can I come?"

"Oh," Mom said, her hands fluttering. "No, no, I don't think so. You'd have to miss school."

"I could help you," Cass said cajolingly. "You know, you always say two heads are better than one. I'm good at remembering details and taking notes and stuff."

Mom rubbed her forehead.

"I don't know. Maybe."

ᘒ

Cass made the coffee in the morning before Mom was up. She put out the cereal and milk and laid a place for Mom with a spoon and napkin. When the alarm clock rang, and Mom crawled out of her side of the bed, Cass handed her a mug of coffee with milk and sugar.

"Bless you, my child."

At eight o'clock, Mom didn't say anything about Cass getting ready to go to school, so Cass didn't bring it up either. Just before eight-thirty, Mom gathered her purse and coat, so Cass got her coat too. Then they headed downstairs to the pavement outside.

At exactly eight-thirty, a black car pulled up, and a man climbed out of the front seat.

"Denise Foster?"

"Yes." Cass could tell Mom was trying to keep her voice from shaking.

"I'm Dan Jacobs. You can call me Dan. I'm here to drive you into town."

"Thanks," said Mom.

He opened the door for them. The inside of the car was all creams and grays and silvers. Cass had never sat on anything so soft. She stretched her legs out, thinking suddenly of Mom's story of being long-lost royalty. Maybe it was really true! Maybe they were going to find out they had a million dollars.

What could you do with a million dollars? Buy a mansion? Go on a 'round-the-world cruise? Buy a private jet? Or maybe they would simply find a little place to live that was near a lake, like the one in her daydream that made music like chimes. Cass spent so much time thinking about all of the options that she scarcely noticed the highway at all, or the downtown streets with glass-filled skyscrapers on all sides.

Then, suddenly, Dan was opening the back door, and she was climbing out after Mom.

"Head up to the sixteenth floor, suite 302," said

Dan. He smiled and shook both their hands. "I'll be waiting for you when you're ready to go."

Mom nodded, looking a little glassy-eyed.

"Come on." Cass held the door for her, found the elevator, pushed the buttons. A few minutes later, she turned the knob of suite 302.

A smartly dressed woman sat behind a curving desk.

"Hello! Is this the lawyer's office?" Cass asked. Her voice sounded too loud in this muted, elegant office. She thought suddenly of the bullies, and how they called her "Greasy Hair."

Mom fumbled with the envelope. "Maracle and Brant?"

The lady smiled. "Are you Denise Foster, by any chance?"

Mom nodded dumbly.

"Welcome! I am so glad to meet you. Ms. Maracle has been waiting for you."

☙

Ms. Maracle stood up when they walked in. She stepped quickly around the desk and shook both their hands. Then she gestured to seats, and they all sat together on the same side of the desk.

14

"Thank you for coming," said Ms. Maracle. "Coffee or tea?"

"Oh, I don't know," said Mom. "Nothing."

"A nice cup of tea," Ms. Maracle said cajolingly. "Something warm after your trip."

Mom sort of nodded and shrugged at the same time, pretty much on the verge of losing it. Cass squeezed her hand hard and didn't let go.

"And maybe some apple juice for this young lady." Ms. Maracle smiled at her warmly, and Cass had the sudden feeling that things would be okay. She liked the lawyer's gentle face. Ms. Maracle wouldn't, couldn't do anything to hurt Mom.

A little while later, when everyone had something to drink near at hand, Ms. Maracle opened up a file on her lap.

"Well, now," she said. "Here it is. The last will and testament of Maria Elizabeth Burns." She leaned forward kindly toward Mom. "As we talked about on the phone, it is proved beyond doubt that she was your biological mother. I have all of the papers here to answer any questions you might have about that."

Mom crossed her arms.

"And," said Ms. Maracle, "she left everything to you."

15

"I'm not planning to take it," said Mom in a small, tight voice.

"She left you her house," said Ms. Maracle.

She let that sink in.

"And the sum of eleven thousand dollars."

Mom said at last, in the cold voice again, "I waited. I waited for years. On my birthday, Christmas—every time I moved to a new family—I imagined she'd come to get me." Her voice got colder still. "This house and this money, give them to the poor. I don't need them."

"That is your choice, of course," said Ms. Maracle. "And you don't need to decide today. Take some time."

She reached inside the file again. "One other thing. There is a letter for you. Sealed."

She handed it to Mom, who held it limply in her hands.

"Where—where is this house?" Cass's voice sounded funny in her ears, like rocks in a landslide, scraping against each other. "Should we at least go and see it?"

Ms. Maracle said quickly, "That's an excellent idea. Dan can run you over. It's very close."

"I don't need her house."

"Not to have it, just to see it," Cass said. She put her hand on Mom's shoulder, suddenly feeling again like she was the older one.

Then Mom was rubbing her forehead, and Ms. Maracle was taking keys out of an envelope. She handed them to Cass.

"I haven't agreed to anything," Mom reminded them both.

chapter three

Cass kept sneaking looks at Mom in the car as Dan Jacobs drove. Mom looked like wildebeests were marauding through her mind. Cass couldn't begin to imagine what Mom could be feeling. What would it be like for Cass to go to see a house that Mom had left to her after abandoning Cass as a baby?

But Mom hadn't abandoned Cass, never would. Mom had raised Cass alone, without help, without finishing school, without money, working horrible jobs with bullying bosses. And you hardly ever saw anything but a smile on Mom's face. Except today.

Mom reached over and took Cass's hand. She squeezed it and did the I-love-you eyes. Cass squeezed back hard, relief flooding her. They would be okay after this weird day. No matter what happened, no matter where they ended up. If Mom was there with Cass, it would all work out.

Dan's voice broke in on them. "There it is. The developers wanted her to sell, but she refused."

Cass looked out the window at last. They were driving along an avenue with green lawns on each side. Green lawns leading up to homes made of bricks. Porches wide and ornate and the same from house to house. Garages that were all the same, but with differently colored doors.

The people here were rich. Mom was right: they did not belong here.

But Dan was pointing ahead, toward a cul-de-sac at the end. There stood a much older house. It was a single story, crouching as if it were the most stubborn thing ever. Practically buzzing with attitude, a green and white spitfire with a dirt driveway, a maple tree, and bedraggled pink and white flowers. It didn't care that it was nothing like the others. It would hold its ground against them, and they could just back off.

Dan pulled into the dirt driveway, up to the white gate that was in the center of a tough little fence. A minute later he was opening the car door for them, and Cass and Mom were climbing out.

"Take your time, Ms. Foster."

"Oh, we won't be long," Mom said. She put her arm around Cass, and Cass put her arm around Mom. Together they walked up the dirt driveway, past the garden of pink and white flowers.

Mom undid the latch on the gate and swung it wide. It squealed, hinges badly in need of some oil.

Cass followed Mom through the gate and found herself in a backyard that was not really a backyard. It was more like an explosion of colors, most of them wild and out of control. There was something about the confusion of weeds and waving wildflowers that made Cass feel suddenly happy, almost in the way that her daydream about the lake did. It was just a wilder, crazier happiness.

"Come on!" Mom completely surprised Cass by taking off down the hill, purse bouncing off her shoulder. Cass raced after.

At the end of the yard was a small river. After that was the fence marking the end of the property.

And beyond that was—garbage.

There was a sea of it: plastic bags lying on top of each other, along with broken chairs, thrown-away toys, diapers. It was a dumping ground, a no-man's-land at the bottom of the ravine, where people had obviously been tossing stuff they didn't want anymore.

Mom started laughing, kind of hysterically. She laughed harder and harder, until she was snorting and wiping moisture away from her eyes. "She left me a dump!"

Then Mom crumpled the envelope she was holding, the sealed letter Ms. Maracle had given her. She pulled her arm back and threw the envelope as far as she could. The envelope soared in an arc against the blue sky, against the wheeling birds above. Finally, it curved down and landed in the heart of the garbage, out of sight.

"Mom!"

Mom's laughing turned into another sound, kind of strangled. "That's where garbage belongs—in the dump."

"What if it isn't garbage?" Cass cried.

"There is nothing she could say," said Mom, "that I need to hear." She started back up the hill, turned, and stretched out her hand. "Coming?"

Cass hurried after, sighing.

03

The key turned surprisingly easily in the lock. Mom pushed the door open as if it were the entrance to a tomb. Cass followed, keeping close, half-thinking something might jump out, or Mom might faint or something.

But it was a quite ordinary blue and white kitchen that waited for them, tidy and matter-of-fact. It fit that self-reliant little house. Cass liked it right away. She could see herself doing homework at the table while Mom heated stuff up on the stove. And maybe a radio would be playing, while darkness began to fall outside and the kitchen glowed bright and warm. They'd eat at the table with placemats, while Cass told Mom about school, and Mom told Cass about work. School had no bullies in it, and Mom's work was teaching—the thing she'd always wanted to do.

One doorway opened into a small living room. It held a couch and chairs that seemed to have been waiting for someone to sit there. There was a shelf with books, and a fireplace. Suddenly Cass could imagine that it was raining or snowing outside, and she was curled up on that couch with a book while logs crackled and sizzled in the fireplace.

The other doorway led into a hallway. Cass stopped right away, head raised.

What was that?

It was more like a vibration than a sound, either so high or low that her ears couldn't quite catch it. Like a hum, kind of. A mischievous purr.

Cass shook her head, but the cheeky non-sound was still there. She took a tentative step into the hallway. The hum grew a tiny bit. It was like that game when people said "warmer" or "colder." Cass was warmer.

She took another step, and the hum called her to come closer. So she inched along the hallway past other doors, till she was in front of a room.

Ha! The hum was more like a song now, but nothing she could put her finger on. Maybe it was a voice on the wind, maybe it was several voices, but it was as if they were singing somewhere else and Cass was hearing only the shadow of it. Or the memory.

She pushed open the door, and those cheeky non-voices buzzed out a welcome, as if it were a surprise party and she was the main guest. There was trickery in those voices, but something old too, somehow, and trustworthy. Could you be tricky and trustworthy at the same time?

Cass shook her head again. The bullies were right. She was crazy!

Stupid bullies, the mischievous voices seemed to sing. They don't know anything!

"That's the first sign you're crazy," Cass said out loud to the room before her. "You don't think you are."

She stepped in, and those voices chorused triumphantly, telling her she had made it, she had found the treasure.

It was a bedroom. Cass ran her hand over the bed with the multicolored quilt, touched the dresser and mirror tentatively. Cass had never had a bedroom before, and never a bed by herself. Not that she minded sleeping with Mom. It was comforting to have Mom beside her after another day at school, warm proof there was one other person in the world who knew and loved her.

There was a closet too, where you could hang up things. And it even had hangers in it!

The voices swirled around those hangers, singing about how sturdy they were, how good they were at hanging things.

Cass rubbed her forehead.

Part of her loved it so much already that she felt she already lived here.

But rooms were not supposed to sing at you!

The non-voices curled around her, like a hug from friends who knew they could be annoying but were sure you'd be on their side all the same. Friends who knew you'd see past all of their weirdness.

24

"You wouldn't be lonely here," they hummed cheerfully.

Cass rolled her eyes. That was for sure. It would be downright crowded.

CR

When she walked back along the hall, she went slowly again. This time, though, it was because she was trying to think of what she could possibly say to Mom that would convince her they needed to live here.

Mom was looking in the little storage cupboard beside the fireplace, where logs were piled neatly.

She stood up, saw Cass's face.

"Don't fall in love."

"You could go back to school," Cass said softly. "You could become a teacher. For real."

"I can't take her house."

"But she's not here." Cass waved around. "This could be our house, not hers."

"No. We have lives. People don't just give up their lives."

Cass debated inside her head. Then she decided to say it, in the most loving voice she could.

"We don't actually have lives."

Mom was still.

25

"You're in between jobs, you said it yourself. I'm running away from bullies every day. I don't know about you, but I won't be too sorry to say good-bye to that apartment. This place has a living room and bedrooms and a fireplace."

Cass's voice got stronger because Mom wasn't arguing. She was just standing there.

"And there might be a dump at the end of the yard, but there's green back there too, and flowers, and—and trees and birds. It's a lot better than garbage cans and sidewalks and cars all the time, everywhere you go. And I bet the school's nicer here, and I bet there's better jobs."

She raised her chin, feeling just as scrappy as the little house, buoyed by the encouraging non-voices that urged her on.

"And I want to live here."

chapter four

The cube van inched along, while Mom leaned forward and squinted through the windshield, gripping the wheel as though their lives depended on it. Cass figured she could probably run beside the van and hardly be out of breath. Still, since Mom hadn't driven at any time during Cass's life, maybe it was best for her to take it slowly. Cass had been surprised to learn she had a license at all.

"You turn right up there."

Mom frowned at the windshield, her nose practically an inch away from it. "Are you sure?"

"And then you turn left on that fancy street, and the house is at the end."

27

"I thought—" said Mom. And then she couldn't talk anymore because she had to concentrate.

Mom had agreed to use just enough of the money left to her in the will to rent the van. The rest had gone into a trust fund for Cass. The house was Cass's too, or at least Ms. Maracle said she'd set it up so it would be when Cass was old enough. Cass still couldn't believe any of it was happening.

Soon they were creeping along the street with the big houses, and the stubborn little white and green house was ahead of them. But now, Cass thought, it was saying "Finally!" as if it had been waiting forever for them to get there.

Mom managed to turn the cube van into the driveway and crawled toward the house before jerking on the brakes, sending them both forward as if they were bowing to the house.

Cass snorted with laughter.

Mom shot her a look, exhaled loudly, and turned off the engine.

A minute later, Cass unlocked the door to the little blue kitchen.

"Our kitchen," she said out loud. "Our sink, our cupboards, our countertops. Our fridge."

"Our kitchen stuff," Mom said, puffing and dumping

a box on the floor. "Come on, there's lots more to go!"

Cass helped Mom lift out bags and suitcases. They piled them on the lawn next to the flower garden. Although it wasn't a hot day, sweat was soon pouring down Cass's forehead.

"Hello! I've brought you some water."

It was a man's voice, cheerful and hearty. He was striding across the lawn from the house next door, wearing faded jeans and a T-shirt that said *Super Teacher*. He was carrying two glasses and grinning widely. "Thought I'd be the first to welcome you to the neighborhood."

Mom looked at him somewhat distrustfully, then smiled slightly and took a glass of water. Cass eagerly reached for the other one.

"Thanks," Mom said, not looking him in the eye.

"Don't mention it." He pointed to himself. "Dave Gregor."

Mom cleared her throat as if her voice suddenly wasn't working right. "Denise Foster," she mumbled, still looking past him. Then she was silent, gripping the glass of water and staring into it.

"I'm Cass."

"Welcome!" If Mr. Gregor was taken aback at the unfriendliness of Mom's behavior, he didn't show it at all. "I just moved in right over there a couple of weeks ago, me and my bulldog, Bessie. She's a mush head, but I thought I'd keep her inside till I found out if you liked dogs or not. She won't bother you, I promise. Doesn't bark much. Loves kids…" His voice ground down as he watched Mom's face. "You don't like dogs, do you?"

"I don't mind them," Mom lied. Cass knew all about it. In one of the foster homes, there had been a German shepherd that used to corner Mom on the stairs and scared the living daylights out of her.

"I'll keep her out of your way," Mr. Gregor promised. "Though she's a really good girl. Honestly, she wouldn't hurt a fly."

He looked around somewhat helplessly, as Mom was not really communicating back at all, although she was nodding at his words. His eyes hit on the pile of boxes and bags. "Here, let me help you with these."

"Oh, no, we don't need—" Mom was saying. But Mr. Gregor hoisted up a suitcase. He grinned down at Cass, who couldn't help but like him. "Where do I put this?"

"Kitchen," Cass said.

"Show me the way, kid."

Mr. Gregor came back out to the van after he had dumped the first load. Mom was continuing to put things on the lawn and seemed to be very preoccupied with doing that.

"So, what do you do?" Mr. Gregor asked her, clearly determined to push ahead with a conversation even though—by the way Mom was acting—she had apparently forgotten that he was there. "Me, I teach at the elementary school down the street." He indicated his shirt. "See? Super Teacher. The kids got me that a couple of years ago."

"Mom's—in between jobs," Cass said.

"Just for now," Mom said to the box she was carrying. "Not for long."

"Any idea what kind of work you're looking for? Maybe I can help, if you want to give me your résumé. I've taught a lot of kids and know a lot of families."

Mr. Gregor was smiling at Mom with nothing but goodwill on his face. Mom shot him a look that could have meant anything. "Okay, maybe," she said.

Cass picked up the suitcase with her clothes in it and headed back inside, leaving them there to work it out.

It was time to see her room again. And now it really was hers.

Just like last time, she started to hear that buzzing hum as soon as she set foot in the hallway. Like those voices were trying not to laugh, like they had a surprise in store.

"I know the surprise," Cass told them. "I saw the room already, remember?"

The voices did gymnastics around her, mischievous echoes from far away.

She hauled the suitcase onto the bed and unlatched it. She would find just the right place for every piece of clothing. Which ones would she hang up? Which ones would she put in drawers? And which drawers for which kinds of clothes? Cass had never had all the drawers to herself before.

She turned toward the dresser, and the voices suddenly surged.

"Okay, okay!" Cass told them. Apparently those voices were as excited about putting her clothes away as she was. "Which drawer do you want first?"

She held her hand in front of a drawer. The voices hummed enthusiastically. She hovered by the next one, and they buzzed just a bit more. And Cass was playing right along, getting crazier by the minute, like this was normal.

They practically turned themselves inside out when her hand stopped next to the first drawer on the right-hand side.

"You like this one?" Cass asked the voices.

She slid the drawer open.

There was something in tissue paper. Cass pushed the paper back to reveal what was inside.

Then she screamed.

ଔ

They came running, Mom and Mr. Gregor.

Mom hugged her hard. "What's wrong, my darling? What happened?"

Cass was feeling stupid now, sitting on the floor, heart still beating fast. "In the drawer. Sorry. It scared me."

She didn't mention how the voices had swelled almost to a triumphant yell in her head, and how she'd realized they were coming out of the thing that was in the drawer. That thing had been singing to her all along.

Mr. Gregor was peering into the drawer with some kind of awe on his face.

"I think it's a false face."

Cass slowly got to her feet and approached the drawer again. The voices had backed off a little now, as if they realized they had scared her. They were friends, not enemies.

Mom was staring at it. "It's an *ugly* face."

"False face. An Iroquois healing mask," Mr. Gregor

said. "There's a large Aboriginal population around here. I don't mean to be personal—are you of Aboriginal descent?"

"No."

Cass was inching closer, and she reached out her hand to the mask. She couldn't quite touch it yet.

The face was carved from some kind of wood, mis-shapen, its mouth curving up into a kind of distorted, knowing half-smile as if it held all of the strange jokes of the universe inside. Its eyes were not quite circles, not quite ovals, not even quite the same size. What they were, though, was brilliant, uncanny white against the red of the face. If they could move, Cass thought, they would be rolling, looking at everything at once. The forehead was all wrinkles, like that mask was planning something huge. And framing that otherworldly face was a mass of crazed black hair, piled inside the tissue paper that had been cradling the mask.

Cass stared at it, hardly able to tear her eyes away. She had the strangest feeling that she almost recognized it. The mask grinned back knowingly as if it could see inside her too.

"Hot, hot, hot!" sang the voices. She had found where they were hiding. She had won the game.

chapter five

By the time they'd unloaded everything and hauled it into the house, Mom was starting to talk to Mr. Gregor like he wasn't a threat to her. And when he ordered them a welcome pizza, she didn't turn it down outright.

So they all ate around the little kitchen table, surrounded by boxes and bags, while the light began to gradually fade outside, and the kitchen glowed warmer and warmer. Mr. Gregor told them funny stories about his students. Like about the time they all came in walking backward and sat backward in their chairs. So he taught the class from the back of the room, facing the wall, until nobody could keep from laughing.

Mom was laughing too by the end, her face lit up and her eyes bright in the way Cass loved. Like nothing bad had ever happened, like Mom hadn't learned to be scared of everyone who came along. She was the hopeful, joyful Mom who came out only when it was safe.

At last, when it was quite dark, Mr. Gregor stood up and said, "Well, I hate to leave this welcome party, but Bessie will be waiting for her supper, so I must go!"

"Thanks for your help," Mom said, not looking at his face, suddenly shy again. "And the pizza."

"It was great!" Cass said with huge enthusiasm, to make up for Mom.

Mr. Gregor started carrying plates over to the little counter.

"No, leave it!" Mom said, jumping up.

Mr. Gregor ignored her, picking up the glasses next. He asked Cass, "Are you starting school tomorrow? If so, I'll see you there."

An electric shock ran through Cass.

School.

"No biggie," said Mr. Gregor lightly. "You can ignore me in the halls, I can take it!"

"No, no," said Cass. She couldn't think of anything to say after that, though. It was too big, and too horrible.

"Cass has had a rough time at schools. There's been a lot of bullying." For the first time, Mom was looking right at Mr. Gregor, with all her helplessness and love for Cass all over her face, making Cass adore her more than she thought was possible. "It never seems to get any easier."

Mr. Gregor studied Mom's face. He looked from Mom to Cass. Then he nodded. He got down in a squatting position in front of Cass, who was still sitting in her chair. He looked her in the eye. "I'm making you a promise, Cass. It's going to get easier now."

Cass flushed.

"Tomorrow," said Mr. Gregor, "will be a piece of cake. That's a guarantee. Whatever flavor you like. You and me, we'll take them all on."

His eyes crinkled at her, and for a second, she almost believed him.

ଓ

Before Cass got into bed, she opened the drawer. That drawer. She pushed back the tissue paper. She and the mask looked each other in the eye.

"I think I like you," Cass said after awhile. "But let's not go too far."

Too late, the voices seemed to sing, filled with sat-isfaction at their own funny selves, pleased with the mischief they had played while hiding and being found. Now they had a new playmate, and they darted around Cass as if they were strings binding her. But friendly strings, friendlier than what waited tomorrow.

Later Mom tucked her in, hugged her hard, kissed her on the forehead.

"I don't want to go," Cass whispered.

Mom stroked her forehead. "I'll go with you. We'll walk together."

"I hate school. I can't go back."

"Maybe it'll be different," Mom said helplessly. "With Mr. Gregor there, I mean. He said he wouldn't let anything happen."

But Cass knew how it worked. Bullies did things only when teachers weren't there. And Mr. Gregor couldn't be there every minute of every day, nobody could.

"All we can do," Mom said gently, "is start again. Over and over, as many times as we have to. And be brave. We can't change what is coming, but we can face it with courage. You are my girl who doesn't give up, no matter what. You are my powerful Cass."

Mom's words resonated in Cass's head as she began to drift toward sleep. They mingled with the song of the mask. As Cass grew sleepier, the mask seemed to support Mom's words like a cradle of sounds, woven together to keep Cass safe in the night.

"You are not alone," the mask seemed to be chanting, softly, softly.

And then she was dreaming.

☙

She was tiny, dwarfed by an enormous brick school, three or four stories high, with what looked like a bell tower on top. A series of balconies climbed above the front door, like cages.

Something was pushing her toward it, some unkind force that swept her up the stairs to the big front doors and would tolerate no refusal. It was larger than her, larger than anyone, and she couldn't fight it because she couldn't really see or understand it. But somehow she knew that when she was taken inside, it would not let her out for years. It would not let her be with Mom. Mom was not good for her anymore.

The doors opened, and although she fought, she was inside. Faces loomed everywhere, wide eyes like her own.

They were all animals being groomed for something. For a show, maybe. They would not be free creatures anymore, because free meant wild.

☙

She woke up sweating, all tangled up in bedsheets and the multicolored quilt. Her heart was pounding so hard it was like a drum against her chest. She opened her eyes, hoping it was still dark. But sunshine flooded the little room.

It was tomorrow.

She squeezed her eyes tightly shut again. *Go away, go away!*

Gradually she realized that the mask was singing to her. It had maybe never stopped, all night long. The voices darted around her, like specks of light. They were singing about the children in her dream, with the terrified eyes. The voices were calling out to them, comforting. But they were calling to Cass too.

"Be strong, be brave! Do not forget about yourself!" they chanted, looping about Cass like an incantation.

"How could I forget about myself?" Cass said aloud.

☙

Mom surprised her with oatmeal and brown sugar, Cass's favorite. They ate side by side in the little kitchen, while Cass's stomach did loops and twirls. It felt like her last meal before being executed. Then Mom washed the dishes, while Cass brushed her teeth and got her shoes on.

"Ready, sunshine?" Mom shrugged on her coat and grabbed her purse, a hopeful smile pasted on her face.

"No." Not even with oatmeal warm in her stomach and a mask singing in her head and Mom doing the I-love-you eyes.

But she followed Mom anyway, down the dirt driveway and along the sidewalk, past the huge houses and the ornamental bushes. Other kids had started walking too, in pairs and trios, carrying backpacks. They'd all probably be chasing Cass home tonight.

It was a quick walk to the school, just one turn and there it was, nestled in a green field and looking nothing like the school in her dream. On the far side, the road led to a downtown with little shops, the kind of place where people strolled and had coffee. Unlike Cass, who was going to jail.

ℭℛ

The secretary looked up as Mom and Cass walked into the office.

"Good morning," Mom said, standing stiffly, with a voice that barely shook. "I need to sign up my daughter for school."

The secretary shuffled through a filing cabinet, bringing out some papers. "We'll need to get you to fill these out. Have you got your supporting documents with you?"

"My—" Mom looked at Cass helplessly. "What do I need?"

The secretary turned the computer monitor around so she could see. "It's all online at the school board website."

Mom flushed. "I'm sorry. I didn't know. I don't have a computer."

"Oh!" said the secretary, as if Mom had just said that she didn't have a stove.

Just then, the office door swung open. In strode Mr. Gregor, carrying a briefcase and whistling. "Good morning, Sheila!"

Then he noticed Cass and Mom. His face broke into a smile.

"Welcome! Getting all registered?"

"I—I don't know," Mom said, getting flustered and rummaging in her purse. "I don't know if I have my supporting documents."

Mr. Gregor said smoothly, "Well, Sheila, what do we need? Proof of address? Birth certificate?"

For the next several minutes, Mr. Gregor kept up a light level of chatter while helping Mom to figure out what she needed and simultaneously making subtly funny faces at Cass, as if this was all a ridiculous series of hoops they had to jump through. At last, Mom filled out the forms and it was all done. Cass's life was signed away again.

Mr. Gregor conferred with the secretary quietly. Then he said gently, "Cass, I'll take you down to meet your teacher. Come on, it'll be okay."

Helplessly, Cass looked imploringly at Mom. Water sprang to her eyes.

Mom hugged her and held on for a long time. "You will be just fine, sweetheart."

"Be brave," sang something else, just on the threshold of Cass's hearing.

She breathed in slowly, and out again.

Mr. Gregor held the door open for her and she walked through.

chapter six

When the bell rang, Cass was already crouched in her chair. Ms. Clemens, Cass's new grade-six teacher, had allowed Cass to pick out a place where her new desk would be put, so Cass had chosen a location as far away as possible from the front of the room. Ms. Clemens had grouped the desk with two others.

"We'll try it for today," Ms. Clemens had said kindly. "If you don't feel comfortable there, we can always change it." She had chatted with Mr. Gregor for several minutes in the hall, and Cass was pretty certain Mr. Gregor had told Ms. Clemens about the bullies.

Great, now all of the teachers would be feeling sorry for her, on top of everything else.

The kids burst into the room, shouting and laughing, scraping chairs to desks, slamming backpacks down. Cass shrank further and concentrated on rubbing her fingers together under the desk.

"Hey, who are you? Are you new or something?"

It was a stocky boy with red hair and surprisingly fine features, a light sprinkling of freckles over his nose. Brows drawn together, clever eyes, trying to figure Cass out.

She nodded, voice caught in her throat. "Y-y-yes."

The boy threw himself heavily into the desk beside hers. "What's your name?"

"Cass. Uh, Cass Foster."

"Ellis McCallister. Oh no, that's my mom." He ducked down.

A tall, very well-dressed woman was striding across the classroom to Ms. Clemens. Cass's new teacher stood up from where she had been bending down over a student's desk. The smile she presented to the woman was about the most pathetic imitation of a friendly welcome that Cass had ever seen. Ms. Clemens was almost as bad at faking things as Mom.

"Good morning, Mrs. McCallister," said Ms. Clemens.

The well-dressed lady smiled widely and held out her hand. "So nice to see you again, Ms. Clemens. How have you been?"

"Fine, thanks. And yourself?"

"Very well!" The lady put a hand on Ms. Clemens's arm. "I didn't know if you might have just a minute to speak? Just regarding a question I had about Ellis's social studies quiz? There were a couple of answers I was wondering about, and I was hoping we could revisit them. I have a feeling there might be a couple of marks that you missed. Is this a good time?"

"Well," said Ms. Clemens, gesturing around to the class, as they continued to drag chairs to their desks and loudly take out their materials for the day. "I am just about to start teaching. I'd be happy to talk about Ellis's test, if you wanted to make an appointment for another time...."

"Oh!" said Ellis's mother, penciled eyebrows crawling up her forehead. "Oh, I'm very sorry. I must have misunderstood. I thought parents were encouraged to be part of the education process?"

Ellis groaned slightly and began to slide under his desk, making gestures at his neck as if he wanted to rip his head off.

Ms. Clemens leaned her head close to Mrs. McCallister, and they spoke quietly for a minute. Mrs. McCallister said a number of things back, and although Cass couldn't hear the words, she was sure from the tone that Ellis's mother was not happy.

Ms. Clemens stood straight and raised her chin to the taller woman. She said in a clear, cool voice: "I will be happy to phone you later to arrange something at our mutual convenience."

Ellis's mother looked very displeased, but left a moment later.

Just then, another boy placed a chair in front of the desk opposite to Cass's desk. His dark hair fell forward over his face, and his eyes were looking down, as he sat. He unzipped his backpack, pulled out a notebook, and began to write in small, neat movements, as if he didn't want to draw attention to himself.

Ellis said to Cass, "Watch this." He grabbed the boy's notebook and threw it in front of Cass. "See, this is what you do when you're a loser like Degan."

Cass couldn't help looking at the notebook in front of her. It was covered in little drawings—so many that they obscured the words written there. Branches and vines curled upward around the letters, and amid them a variety of creatures were hidden. A mouse nibbled seeds, a bird nestled in a bed of leaves, rabbits huddled amid roots. Here and there, children climbed up the vines like Jack up a beanstalk.

But the most amazing part was the background, toward the top of the page. There, the boy had drawn mountains with snow glinting off them. And between the mountains was a gleaming lake. It was a lot like the lake in Cass's daydream.

"That's so good!" she said.

The boy flushed and glanced at her quickly. He held out his hand, and Cass put the notebook into it. He placed it on the desk, picked up his pencil, and began to draw again as if neither Cass nor Ellis were there.

Ellis looked annoyed. "No, it's not. It's stupid. It's a waste of time."

"Why do you care so much?" the boy asked in a voice that was calm. He kept drawing. "Why does it matter to you?"

Ellis edged back. "Hey, don't scalp me, Hill, I'm just trying to help you. You gotta learn focus, my friend."

Don't scalp me. Cass looked again at the boy's face.

With his dark hair and brown skin, she wondered suddenly if he was Aboriginal. Mr. Gregor had said there was a large Aboriginal population in the city. She had never seen a Native person before.

Then she felt angry. What a rude thing for Ellis to say!

Something curled around the back of her mind, the merest hint of a voice that sang softly in agreement.

Before she knew it she was sitting up straighter, chin out, just like Ms. Clemens.

"I'm Cass Foster," she said to the boy in the strongest voice she could. "I think you're talented. I think you'll be an artist one day."

The boy glanced up at her from under his fringe of hair; his neutral expression didn't tell Cass what he was thinking. Then he looked down again, hunched over his notebook.

"Don't bother," Ellis told Cass. "He just sits there and draws those stupid pictures all the time. I don't think he even knows English."

"Degan Hill," said the boy in a muffled voice. Then he cleared his throat, shot Cass another wary, darting glance. "That's my name. Degan Hill."

chapter seven

It was an unusual table group, Cass decided. Degan Hill crouched over his notebook, one hand cradling his head, while he scribbled with the other. His eyes were half-closed. He looked like he was almost asleep. Cass would have believed he was, except that his other hand moved swiftly across the page.

Meanwhile, Ellis McCallister could not keep still. He had a collection of small objects on his desk, and he was moving them around. Sometimes he knocked them down while making explosion noises. At other times, he stuck them together with paper clips that he had twisted into small fragments of wire. Cass was fascinated as he skewered together two eraser chunks, some folded paper strips, a pipe cleaner, a broken pencil sharpener and two thumbtacks. Suddenly a little robot emerged from beneath his hands, sturdy and strutting with attitude.

Ellis trotted the robot across his desk while croaking a marching tune. Cass couldn't help snorting. Next, Ellis lifted the robot, squinted, lined it up.

"Activate!"

The robot soared through the air and hit Degan squarely in the forehead. Degan shot to his feet, startled, with a hand to his head.

"Sorry! Sorry!" Ellis scrambled to retrieve the robot from the floor by Degan's shoe. "I thought you were asleep. Just trying to help."

Degan sat down again, his eyes like coals but saying nothing.

"She thought it was funny," Ellis said, gesturing at Cass.

Cass flushed with guilt. "I did not."

"You were laughing."

Degan flicked a glance at her from under his hair.

Cass said fiercely, "I would never laugh to see someone hit someone else. I was only laughing when you made the robot go across the desk."

"I didn't mean to hit him, I was just keeping him

awake," Ellis said reasonably. "I already said that. It was a mercy mission."

"Leave me out of it," Cass snapped, hardly able to believe the strong words coming out of her mouth. Then she hunched down, her nose almost on her work. Her insides were turning over horribly. Ellis would go after her now, she was sure of it.

But he went back to humming and assembling the pieces into a little truck, complete with wheels made of the wrestled-off metal ends of pencils.

Something rose up inside her, like faraway memories of voices calling in triumph. As if the mask knew what she had done, knew how much bravery it had taken, and hailed her.

෨

At recess Degan shot out of his chair, notebook in his hand. Although their table group was almost at the back of the room, he was the first out of the classroom. Cass understood. She had always tried to get a head start before the bullies could follow.

She wanted to tell Degan that. She wanted him to know she wasn't like Ellis.

Outside, she stood on the pavement and looked

around. Unfamiliar kids ran everywhere. Cass crossed her arms and started to walk in no particular direction, eyes down but still searching for the boy with the fringe of dark hair who would probably have found a place as far out of sight as possible. That was what Cass would have done, after all.

"Hey, Cass! I was hoping I'd see you."

Mr. Gregor fell into step beside her, beaming down. "Confession time: I was actually looking for you. Have to know how it's going this morning. Everything okay?"

She flushed, thinking about Degan. "Yes!" she said brightly.

Except it wasn't.

Except someone thought *she* was a bully. And she had to let him know she wasn't, that she knew what it was like to be the victim and she could never stand by and watch it happen to someone else. She wasn't like Ellis!

"What did you do in class? Did you meet any kids?"

Somehow words came out of her mouth, but she wasn't really paying attention to them. And Mr. Gregor was chatting back, but she wasn't really noticing his words either.

"And your mom, what's she up to today?"

Cass came back to the conversation. "I think she's looking for a job."

"Ah," said Mr. Gregor. "Can you please tell her again that I'd be happy to look over her résumé? I really do know a lot of people besides Bessie."

"I will."

At that moment, a kid stopped them. "Mr. Gregor, that guy over there fell down and he's crying."

"Excuse me," Mr. Gregor said to Cass.

"See you later," Cass said.

She walked quickly past everything. Degan had to be around somewhere. The trouble was, it was hard to look for him without looking at everyone else. So she kept glancing up and down, heart bouncing in her chest.

She found him at last, around the back of a portable, hunched against it with knees drawn up. His head was bent over the notebook, and his hand moved swiftly, sketching something.

Cass stood there in front of him, trying to figure out what to say. Just then, a figure bounced up beside her.

"So this is where everybody went!" Ellis shouted.

Cass jumped and let out a sound that was part frustration and part terror. He had followed her!

"Please leave me alone. I'm not bothering either of you. I'm just drawing." Degan spoke in a soft, level voice that reminded Cass of the distant rumble of thunder.

In one smooth gesture, Ellis leaned down and

grabbed the notebook. However, his fingers slipped, and the book turned like a wheel, flying out of his hands.

All three stared as it arced in the air and dropped down, directly into a puddle.

Cass leaped forward and retrieved the notebook from the puddle. It was dripping wet with mud. She wiped it on her coat, both sides.

"I'm so sorry," she gasped. All the words she had hoped to say about not being a bully were now scrambled in her head. She stared helplessly at the notebook. The picture was half-covered in a brown smear.

Even under the mud, though, she could see what he had been drawing. There was a man crouched on a cliff, maybe ready to fly or to dive. His face was twisted, with eyes not quite the same size, and a lopsided, smiling mouth. Masses of hair floated around his face.

She drew in breath sharply. Something in the man's face was very much like her mask.

"I didn't mean to," Ellis said.

Ellis grabbed the notebook again, but she held on. She winced, expecting him to hit her now, but she couldn't let him have it.

R-r-r-rip!

Then her eyes were filled with tears as she stared at the book in her hand. Ellis had torn out half the pages.

The man on the cliff had been ripped in two.

Ellis stared at the pages in his fist too, as if he couldn't quite believe what he was holding.

Degan said in a low voice to Ellis: "It doesn't matter to you, does it? It doesn't matter what I think or what I am inside. I'm just a target to you, just a joke you keep making."

Ellis looked stung at this. He frowned, and Cass could see him trying to think what to say back.

"Well, at least my family pays taxes," Ellis snapped at last, "unlike you, you Indian."

chapter eight

Cass walked quickly away from the school, arms crossed, heart pounding. She kept seeing Degan's face when the pages of his notebook ripped in her hands. She had helped Ellis to be a bully again, although she hadn't meant to. She had destroyed that astonishing picture of the man on the cliff, who pulsed with the power of choice—to fly or to fall.

Inside, faintly, almost like a beat that wouldn't stop, the mask voices seemed to agree. They vibrated with regret, with sorrow. They were inside her head, resounding in her heart. She could hardly bear their disappointment.

And then she heard it.

"Yeah, head back to your tepee, whatever. I don't even care."

It was Ellis's voice, raised in defiance, not far behind her.

Was he talking to her?

But then came Degan's voice. "Why are you following me?"

"We go home this way, in case you'd forgotten," someone else called. "Except we don't turn on King Street and go to the criminal side of town like you do."

Cass shrugged into her coat, like a turtle trying to get its head into its shell. So Ellis had at least one other person with him, maybe more.

The mask's pulsing voices kept thumping inside her, calling to her, telling her to turn around.

I can't, she thought. *Ellis hasn't seen me. I can get away if I keep walking.*

"I didn't mean to wreck your stupid notebook," Ellis said. "I don't even know why you keep drawing that stuff all the time. It's not like you're ever going to get a job from it or make money. It's a waste of time."

Several voices laughed.

The pounding grew inside Cass.

Before she could think about it more, before she could tell herself not to, she swung around.

Ellis had three boys with him. Degan was walking a few paces in front of them, head down, hands in the pockets of his coat—like if he tried hard enough, he could become invisible.

Cass fell into step beside Degan, who was ignoring her. He probably thought she was going to join in the bullying.

"Hey!" she heard herself saying to Degan brightly, like she hadn't wrecked his notebook, like they were friends. "I just wanted to say: I think you're an amazing artist. How did you learn to draw like that? I wish I could draw. Maybe you can show me sometime."

Degan said nothing.

"I guess some other people must be pretty jealous of that," Cass went on. "Because they can't draw and everything. But we can't all be good at stuff, right, Ellis?"

She whirled around on Ellis and his friends.

"Don't worry, you'll find something you're good at. Everybody's good at something. Everybody's got a talent. Just keep trying."

"What is your problem?" Ellis said, looking confused and fierce.

"I haven't got a problem," Cass said, head whirling, riding on a wave of adrenaline, sure she was going to crash at any moment. "Just walking with my friend.

59

Just walking home. Did you know Mr. Gregor is my neighbor? He's probably going to drive along here any minute."

"I'm good at lots of things," Ellis said.

"You should go do them," Cass said, while the beat inside her kept growing. "You should go do them right now."

Then everything got very quiet. The whole world seemed to stop. It was just Cass and the four of them, the four bullies. And she was not going to look away first.

At last Ellis kicked a stone across the road, frowning at it.

"Come on," he said to the other boys, voice high. "We don't need to talk to a girl."

☙

Degan was far up the street now, moving fast. Cass sprinted till she was beside him, then slowed to his pace.

"Please go away," Degan said, walking faster. "I just want to go home. I'm just trying to go home."

Words burst out of her. "I'm sorry about the note-book. I was trying to keep him from taking it again, then it ripped. It was—it was the most beautiful drawing. I couldn't take my eyes off it. I didn't know what he was

60

planning to do—to take off into the sky, or jump, or just stay crouched like he was hiding."

Degan looked at her sideways.

"I will figure out how to buy you a new sketch book or to fix the old one. I don't have any money right now, but I'll get some, I can get a job doing something like shoveling sidewalks when there's snow, or I could rake leaves…"

Degan said in a low voice: "I don't want a new notepad."

"I'll get you one anyway. I wish I could fix your picture. It was so—so—" She struggled for the words. "So strong. That man deciding what to do. Which way to go."

Degan kept pounding along, while Cass ran beside him.

"Which way would you choose?" Degan said suddenly, stopping to look at her as if this was important.

Cass thought about that man. She thought about what it would be like for him to soar above everything. It was like the daydream she had about being carried on the wind, seeing the lake laid out far below.

"I'd go up," she said. "I'd go so high that everything was tiny below me, so high I was above the birds."

Degan said bitterly: "Maybe he's waiting to pounce. Like Ellis."

"I'm not like Ellis," Cass said desperately. "You don't know. Back at my old school…"

How could she explain it?

"Every day," she said softly. "They used to beat me up every day."

The voices curled around the memory, the fear of it.

"And nobody ever cared. Not the principal, not the teachers. Not the other kids. Sometimes someone would stop them, some stranger. But not for long."

Degan shoved his hands in his pockets and hunched his shoulders. He was listening.

"I guess I can see why they did it," Cass whispered. "Because of my clothes. Because my mom wasn't very rich. Because we went to the food bank." Her voice shook with the memory. "They thought they were better than me, I guess. You can beat up someone you think isn't as good as you."

"No. It wasn't you. There's nothing wrong with you. My aunt says they do it because something's wrong inside them. Something's broken and needs to be fixed. They think they can fix it by hurting other people."

Cass wiped away the tears that had suddenly welled up in her eyes when Degan said that. Nobody had ever told her there was nothing wrong with her, except Mom. And Mom didn't even know most of what had gone on, because Cass hadn't wanted to worry her. She had already told this boy, Degan, more than she had told Mom.

"Come on, let's go," said Degan, and they started walking again, past the big houses that lined Cass's street. It was weird, Cass thought, walking with someone she had only just met. But it felt perfectly normal too. Maybe people who had been bullied had a bond.

They walked in silence for awhile, along the pristine road with the hedges and balconies, past houses in which neither of them might belong. Then, in a hesitant voice, Degan said, "My aunt thinks my generation can be healers. Change the way things are. She tells me to look past now to the future, and then channel the spirit to make it happen."

He looked sideways at her shyly. "That probably sounds weird to you. My aunt's a little out there. She's a healer, she has dreams, people come to her for help."

Cass asked curiously, "Do you think it's weird?"

He laughed, and it was the first time she had seen him smile. "Nah, I grew up with it. Dreams, spirits, healing. Part of our traditional ways."

Dreams and spirits.

It sprang into her head suddenly, that strange dream she had had of the children locked up. She'd forgotten about it until this minute. It had been so real, so soaked in sadness. Like a message, like a call through time.

"Tell me about the traditional ways," she said. "Please."

"What do you want to know?"

The words sprang from her mouth without her planning them.

"About the false faces. The false face masks." She took a deep breath. "I think I have one. I found it in my drawer when we moved in. It's made out of wood. It's got a weird face, with eyes that aren't the same size, and a mouth that's only smiling on one side. It's got all this black hair. Sometimes I think I like it, and sometimes I think it's horrible." She took a breath and decided to trust him with everything. "And I'm dreaming about it too. I think—I think it's trying to send me messages."

Degan didn't laugh at her. "My aunt says you have to be careful with them. They're tricky."

"Tricky…how?"

"Lots of things. My aunt told me about this guy who had two of them, facing each other on two walls of a hallway. They got into all this trouble, moved stuff, turned lights on and off."

"Could a false face…sing?" she whispered.

"Sing?" Degan stared.

"It—it makes music," Cass said. "Not like music. I don't know how to say it. It tells me things. It sings about bullies; it tells me I can be strong."

They were on Cass's driveway now. Degan had not turned onto King Street but had instead walked Cass home.

"Am I going crazy?" Cass whispered.

Degan shook his head, looking impressed. "There's a spirit running through those masks, can go either good or bad, goes back to the very beginning of creation when there was a battle between the creator and another guy. The creator won, but instead of kicking the other guy out, he let him stay as long as he looked after people." Degan shrugged, looking shamefaced. "My aunt tells it a lot better."

"So you actually believe me?"

He shrugged. "I've heard a lot weirder stuff than that. And singing…it goes back forever with us. Songs for everything: war, death, birth, planting, marriage, curing people. But the real question is, Why is it happening to you? What does the mask want with you?"

They were by the kitchen door now.

"Do you want to see it?" Cass asked hesitantly.

chapter nine

Cass unlocked the door and pushed it open. Degan followed behind her into the calm blue kitchen and stood awkwardly, hands in his pockets. It was the strangest thing possible, to be returning home with a kid from school at the end of her first day. Maybe he was even going to be a new friend, something Cass would have never imagined.

There was a note on the kitchen table, with an apple on top of it. A bowl of fruit sat on the table. Mom had been to the food bank.

Hey, sweetness, I'm out returning the cube van and pounding the pavement but will be back probably around the time you get home from school. Hope today was good. I thought about you every minute and sent you heart phone calls! Lots of love, Mom.

"What's a heart phone call?" Degan asked.

Cass blushed. She and Mom had started it ages ago to help with everything. Whenever Mom was down and doubting herself, or Cass was trying to get up the nerve to go back to school, they'd think about the other one so strongly, so lovingly, that they figured that the message was surely being passed between them. It was as if they were linked by a phone connection nobody could see.

"Just—how we support each other," she said. "Mom and me."

"What about your dad?"

"There's no dad. Just us. He left before I was born." She said shyly, "I don't think they were together long. Or maybe at all."

She half-flinched when she checked to see if he was giving her the withering look all of the kids had done at her old school. Looking down on her as if she was less than they were. White trash, they had called her.

But Degan wasn't looking at her that way at all.

He said matter-of-factly, "My aunt isn't really my aunt. She was my mom's best friend. She left the reservation to come and get me after my mom got sick, because she had a dream about it. But then my mom died, and by then my aunt was working as a healer here in the city. So she's raising me here. She thinks that's how it's supposed to go."

It took Cass a minute to take this all in. "What about your dad?"

"He had some problems. There are a lot of reasons. He couldn't help to raise a baby."

Cass stared at Degan, scarcely able to believe how easily he spoke of his parents, amazed that his story was so like her own in parts, but that he hadn't any trace of shame about it. The bullies had shown her so many times that everything about her was something to be ashamed of. But something had prevented Degan from believing that about himself, even though people like Ellis had surely tried to make him feel puny and worthless. What had kept him proud about himself and his background?

"Can I see your mask?"

"Come on."

Cass led the way down the little hallway, listening for the music of the false face, the curling voice so similar to the vines in Degan's sketch. It was pulsing there, at the back of her mind. The mask was pleased she was inviting Degan to see it, happy Cass had met him. Everything was somehow going as the mask thought it should.

But Degan's words echoed in her mind. *You have to be careful with a false face. Those are tricky. It can go either way with them.*

∽

Cass led Degan into her little bedroom, and over to the dresser where the mask lay in the drawer. "It's in here."

She slid the drawer open.

And froze.

It was empty.

"Where is it?" Cass asked.

Degan said nothing.

Then she was frantically pulling out each drawer, rummaging through clothes. She ran to the closet, pulled the door open, tore through everything hanging there.

"It's gone! It's gone!"

But the mask was still singing in her head, far away, like the impossible sound of a finger beckoning.

It was a blur after that. She tore through the house, Degan behind her. She searched in the cupboards of the kitchen, poked through the cushions in the couch, looked in the wood cupboard by the fireplace. There was no sign of the mask.

The panic rose in her as she realized it was not to be found in the house. Where else could it be?

The backyard?

"I'm going to search outside," she said to Degan. Although there was no reason it should be out there. No reason it should have moved at all.

And how did it move? Did someone take it? *Or did it move on its own?*

"Okay," Degan said. His voice was calm. Like it was perfectly normal that they should search outside for a false face that might have gone for a walk. "We'll search outside."

They walked slowly down the slope of the hill, looking behind trees and bushes. Overhead, birds wheeled as if everything was normal. Toward the bottom, they neared the dumping ground that was just beyond the limits of the backyard. The no-man's-land.

Cass climbed the back fence and stepped carefully down into the garbage, seeking out those rolling eyes and that black hair. Instead she saw garbage bags strewn everywhere, along with broken furniture, cracked bottles, and other things nobody wanted.

She almost didn't see the crumpled envelope, lying

where it had landed next to a broken cardboard box. It was bright white against the ground. After a moment's hesitation, Cass leaned down and picked it up, smoothing it out. The typed words on the front were still clearly visible: *Ms. Denise Foster.*

She stood holding it for a minute, trying to decide. Should she leave it where it was, and respect Mom's wish not to know what was in it? Or should she at least bring it back to the house? Should she read it?

No, she couldn't read it—that wouldn't be right.

But, a little voice whispered, *"What if Mom changes her mind one day? What if Mom decides she wants to know what's inside, and you could bring it out for her, kept safe for as long as was needed?"*

Cass stared at it for a minute longer, then shoved the envelope in her pocket.

◌

Mom's excited voice rang out from up the hill.

"Cass? I'm home! Is that you? I have something amazing to show you! What are you doing down there?"

Cass straightened.

"Just—just showing my friend the backyard!" she called, hearing the strangeness of those words. *My friend.*

They climbed up the hill toward Mom.

"Hello," Mom said, glancing from Cass to Degan and back again, with a cautious and then delighted smile that spread across her face. Cass had never brought anyone home before.

"This is Degan Hill," Cass said. "Degan, that's my mom."

"It's a pleasure to meet you!" Mom kept grinning like a fool. She was obviously thrilled and struck with shyness at the same time, wanting to be welcoming but not having much idea how. And meanwhile, all that Cass could think of, desperately, was the mask.

"Hi." Degan shook her hand. Mom beamed even harder, looking flustered.

"Okay, both of you, come on up to the house. I have a big surprise!"

They followed Mom back up the hill and through the gate to the kitchen door. Mom pushed it open and rushed in. Then she stepped to the side of the kitchen table, waved her arm with a flourish, and said, "Ta-da!"

It was a computer. More specifically, it was a big box with a photo of the computer on the front. Mom had opened the top, and Cass could see all of the components inside.

"Wow," Cass breathed. "Is that for us?"

For a minute, she almost forgot about the mask.

Mom nodded, nearly bursting. "There's a printer too. We can use it for so many things. You can do your school-work on it, I can make résumés, and we'll be able to see the school's website and everything! Do you like it?"

"I love it." Cass ran her hand down the side of the box, almost afraid to touch it. They had never owned anything so marvelous before. Other kids had comput-ers, but she had never expected to.

Then a thought occurred to her. "How could we afford this? Aren't computers expensive?"

"That's the best part," Mom said, practically danc-ing. "It didn't cost us a penny. I pawned a few things we didn't need and then I went over and bought the com-puter. It's second hand, but the computer guy said it's certified to be like brand-new."

Degan caught his breath.

At first, she had no idea why. Then a dark feeling crept over her.

But it couldn't be. Mom couldn't have.

"You—pawned a few things? Like what?"

She was afraid to hear the answer.

"Some things left in cupboards that we don't need. Nothing important, don't worry!" Mom could always read Cass's face, and her expression suddenly mirrored the anxiety Cass was feeling inside. "It's okay, my darling!" She put her arm around Cass's shoulders and squeezed reassuringly.

"The mask," Cass said in a tiny voice. "You didn't pawn the mask, did you? The one in the drawer in my room?"

Mom's face got even more worried. She didn't answer for a minute.

"But you didn't like it," she said at last. "It upset you. Don't you remember? It made you nervous." Helplessly she added, "I thought you'd be glad."

Cass's heart was beating so fast that she could hardly see straight. "I loved it! I need it! We have to get it back, Mom! We have to!"

She burst into tears, scarcely able to believe the mask was gone. It couldn't be, because the voice was still singing, deep inside her mind. But now it was the lost cry of one who had been cast away.

Degan was edging toward the door. "I should go home," he said quietly.

Cass hardly heard him.

He closed the door, leaving Mom and Cass alone.

"We have money!" Cass said, her voice shaking. "Can't we use it? Can't we buy the things we need with it, and not pawn my mask?"

Mom sank into a kitchen chair, her face looking aged all of a sudden. Her eyes seemed to droop a little, as if the weight she had inside was too heavy and was pulling her down with it.

"I can't. I can't use it. It's for you, Cass, for when you're older. So I can provide for you in a way that she couldn't—or didn't want to." She breathed out slowly. "I can't explain it very well, but that money is tainted for me. It's—like poison. Too little too late. Some money doesn't make up for the years in those homes, the things that happened."

She put her head in her hands for awhile.

"When I land a job, I will buy it back for you, I promise," she said in a muffled voice.

Mom looked so small and so sad that Cass couldn't even answer, couldn't say everything she needed to say, couldn't explain that she needed the mask so desperately because it sang about soaring above the clouds and the birds, showed her the shining lake below.

She put her arms around Mom instead.

chapter ten

The rest of the evening passed in a kind of fog. Mom struggled with the computer, fiddling with wires and cables and putting them all in the wrong holes while she said things under her breath about how it was broken.

When Mr. Gregor knocked on the door later, he had some extra tomatoes for them because he had bought more than he could possibly use. When he saw the wires everywhere, he ended up offering to put together the computer himself. At first, Mom refused, but after he showed her the first connection, she let him continue. Then he and Mom tried turning it on, and Mr. Gregor ended up teaching Mom about how to get on the

Internet and how to create files. He kept making impossibly bad jokes while he did it. Cass imagined he could probably tame a wild tiger, just through patience and listening and kindness and humor. He seemed almost like someone from another planet, like nothing bad had ever touched him.

But even though he was filling the kitchen with nonsense and laughter, she escaped to her bedroom with homework. It had been too much, a day too filled with things. Starting a new school, standing up to a bully, meeting a possible new friend, and finally—horribly—losing the mask. Not to mention watching Mom crumple like a used newspaper no one wanted, broken and so sad to see Cass unhappy.

Cass hunched on the bed, knees drawn tightly up to her chin, eyes dry but full of unshed tears. Why did she care so much about the mask, anyway? And why did it sing to her still, even when it was gone? It sang of lost things, lost children, lost lives. It didn't make any sense. Who were those children, and why did Cass need to know?

CR

"Cass," Mom called, much later. "Mr. Gregor's leaving."

Cass came out to the kitchen, where the computer was set up at one end of the table. The printer sat beside it, with some paper in it.

"It looks great," she said, trying to make a show of smiling.

Mr. Gregor grinned, standing in the doorway. "I'll give you a lesson on it tomorrow, if you like. You won't take long to pick it up, though." Then his eyes crinkled gently and he added: "I wanted to ask—everything okay at school today?"

"Yes! Why?" Cass said, sounding a little too loud even to her own ears.

"Just checking. I promised things were going to be different at this school. Nobody picking on you? If some-one was giving you a hard time, you'd tell me, wouldn't you?" His face was serious now. "You know I would help."

"Nobody's picking on me," she said. Then she flushed. She wanted to say, *Ellis is picking on Degan, though.* But something stopped her from speaking. Somehow she felt like she needed to clear it with Degan first.

When she crept into bed soon after, she fell asleep almost immediately, exhausted from feelings that rolled and crashed like waves on an unsettled sea. She could feel herself sinking down into a dark hole of forgetting. And then she began to dream.

❦

It started as a song. It was a single voice this time, strong but far away. Cass opened her eyes and sat up. The voice wrapped around her, like the aftereffect of a firework, a thin line of flame that urged her up, up!

Cass climbed out of the bed, following the voice with ears and eyes, watching as it roped around her room, climbed high up the wall then darted through, crying out to her to follow. It was like a battle cry.

She stepped lightly across the room, running her hand hesitantly through the rope of sound. As she did it changed ever so slightly, like ripples in water.

"What do you want?" Cass asked the voice.

She trailed her fingers along the rope, following till it met with the wall. There, instead of touching the solid mass she expected, she discovered that her fingers disappeared out of sight, as if the wall was made of mist.

She was afraid, but pressed harder. Her whole arm vanished smoothly out of sight. Then it was the easiest thing in the world to keep pushing until her whole self emerged into a night brilliant with stars.

Cass stood there, outside the house, with the sky whirling overhead and the very grass seeming to shiver with music she hadn't been able to hear before. The trees, the rocks, the bricks that made up the fancy houses nearby—they rang out with a song that was elemental, that had been forever there, long before people, long before there even had been an Earth.

She could have stood there forever, drinking it in, the wildness of it all. But she could see the voice rippling onward, down the driveway that was wild with pulsing flowers.

The voice wanted her to follow.

So Cass did, stepping hesitantly into a night and a world that was like her own and yet not. This was a world of magic, of uncanny spirits and secrets. Anything might happen here. And she was venturing into it alone, with no one to guide her. No one except the keening voice of the mask.

The voice wound along a path that was her street but not. The houses loomed overhead, but they weren't simply houses. They were all of the things that combined to be houses—living brick and wood and stone, watching her and knowing her under those intelligent stars. Cass followed the voice past them all, then past the school. It wasn't just the school anymore either. It saw her go by, wakeful.

Then she came to a place where there seemed to be stars that had fallen to Earth. Constellations blinked around her, on and off, like fireflies, like gleaming eyes. Cass ran her fingers through them so that the stars rang like chimes.

The voice wove through them, a rope of fire that called to her to push on. Now they came to a tunnel carved out of red rock. Cass held up her hands to feel her way through that knowing darkness, following the voice's battle cry.

She emerged out the other end of the tunnel, and there the world curved, like a huge living snake that showed Cass the way to go. She followed the curve, and it suddenly gave way to a bleak place where the stars were dimmed by cloud that covered the sky. Only the voice glowed here, although thinly through the fog. Things moved around Cass, living beings maybe. She didn't know what they wanted. They might need help, or they might not. If they could see the voice, perhaps they would follow it out of this place. Or maybe they could see and hear it, but could not follow. She was filled with sadness for them, and she wished she could help.

But the voice was ahead of her now, and she hurried to follow. Silently, she sent the message to those shadowy beings: I won't forget you. Someday, somehow she would be back and she would help them.

They climbed up, out of that valley and back into the clear night sky, rising like an arc with the world turning beneath. The voice roped across the heavens and back down again to the living earth.

And all around Cass, suddenly, was a sweetness. It was a smell, a taste. Around her, she sensed others coming together in this place, drawn by the promise of abundance. She wished to stay here too, where things were freely given, where no one would go without. She wanted to go back to those beings in the fog, to tell them about this place. They would be safe here, in the light and in the warmth.

But the voice zoomed past, turned sharply and then came to a wall of living glass and rock. There it stopped, and called her.

Cass raced to catch up.

And her heart leapt.

For there, glowing through the glass, alive, calling to her all along, was the mask. The fire rope of song vanished into its mouth, and the mouth moved now, joyfully singing in its own right.

She had found it!

chapter eleven

When Cass awoke in the morning, she was exhausted, as if she really had traveled all night, following that bright song.

Mom looked even worse than Cass felt. She was sitting in front of the computer, an empty coffee cup beside her and a nearly empty pot of coffee on the counter. Nonetheless, she smiled brightly when Cass stumbled in.

"How long have you been up?" Cass asked. Mom had clearly been typing something, as it was on the screen. She caught the word *Résumé* at the top of it.

Mom ran hands through her hair, yawning. "Just about all night. I wanted to get a résumé written so I could take it around places today." Her voice was excited, even though she was tired. "It could make a real difference in getting a good job, having a résumé. I've never had one before. I was learning all about fonts and things, to make it look professional."

Cass helped herself to toast and sat down beside Mom. She was trying to listen to Mom, but the dream was still fresh in her head, and she could hear the voice of the mask echoing still in her memory. Mom and her résumé almost seemed like a dream, and the dream like reality.

It had been so detailed, so clear. She could remember the stars glowing around her, feel the despair of the beings in the fog, smell the glorious aromas in that place near the mask.

Most of all, she could remember the urgency. The mask was calling to her, and she was desperately following that rope of fire.

"Did you sleep okay?" Mom asked her, yawning again and leaning close to the screen. "Nice dreams?"

Cass thought about telling Mom about the dream. But that would raise the issue of the mask again, and Cass couldn't bear the thought of seeing Mom's face so discouraged and sad. She had decided she wasn't going to mention it again, not if she could help it.

"I don't know," she said awkwardly, biting into her toast.

"I don't often remember my dreams either," Mom said, and she clicked *Print* on the screen. The printer growled to life beside them, and Mom's résumé came rolling out. "How many should I make, I wonder. Maybe twenty? Thirty?"

She squeezed Cass's hand. "Things are changing now. I'm going to get a decent job, something with potential. By the end of the day, I'm going to have interviews lined up."

"I know," Cass said encouragingly. It was so good to see Mom hopeful.

"I forgot to tell you yesterday. Mr. Gregor says if you ever need anything after school, and I'm not here, to go next door. If I'm a little late tonight, he's right there for you." Mom was studying the résumé page, looking for typos.

"Okay. Although I'm old enough to stay on my own."

"I know! Just if you need something. In an emergency." Mom squeezed Cass's hand again. "So you know you aren't alone."

When Cass left the house, Degan stepped out from the maple tree out front.

"Hi!" Cass said, surprised.

"I'm sorry about your mask." He fell into step beside her, and they walked down the dirt driveway to the sidewalk.

"Thanks."

They walked in silence for a minute.

"Are you still hearing it?" he asked. "The music?"

She struggled for a minute, since saying it out loud made it sound impossible. But Degan seemed to be no stranger to unusual things.

"I dreamed about it last night," she said softly. "It was calling me. I had to follow it."

Degan nodded. She immediately felt better. She wasn't crazy if Degan believed her.

"What happened?" he asked. "Where did you follow it?"

Then she told him about everything. The stars, the tunnel, the great snake curling round, the land of mist and fog, the bridge through the sky, the place of plenty, and finally the wall of stone and glass, where the mask shone out at her, alive and mouthing to her.

By the time she was finished, they were almost at school.

"I don't even have the mask anymore," Cass said miserably, "but I'm *still* dreaming about it. I don't know why."

"There's a reason. Dreams aren't just dreams. Not for my people."

"Who are your people?" Cass asked.

"Cayuga Nation. One of the five original nations of the Iroquois confederacy." He spoke simply, but with pride.

"So, what do you think the dream is telling me?"

Degan looked at her sideways, under his fringe of hair. "What do you think?"

"I don't know."

"Really?" Degan flashed a rare grin at her. "Even *I* can tell you what that dream means, and it's not my dream."

"Okay, so what is it telling me, then?"

"Where the mask is, of course."

Cass laughed out loud. "That's crazy. Mom didn't climb into the sky to pawn it. She took it somewhere here in the city. Somewhere she could walk to, since we don't have a car."

Degan let her laugh. When she had stopped, he said, "Dreams talk in codes, in pictures. You have to think hard, meditate on it. The mask is telling you how to find it."

He was about to go on, but at that moment a familiar form came loping across the playground toward them. Red-haired, big, with that fine-featured face. Two other boys ran behind him.

87

"Here he comes," Degan said softly. Not with fear, more with resignation. And something else—pity?

Ellis ran right up in front of them so they couldn't go any farther. Degan stood calmly, with a neutral expression on his face.

"Make it home all right last night?" Ellis asked Degan. "Did she walk you to your door? Sensitive artists need protectors."

Degan didn't answer.

All the old fears were bubbling up in Cass, but she was tired of it. She had walked alone through a strange land last night, following the mask's battle cry. Ellis was nothing compared to that.

"You must be a sensitive artist, then," she said to Ellis.

He stiffened, like there had just been a loud noise. "What are you talking about?"

She gestured to the boys behind him. "You have your protectors too."

Ellis flushed. "They're not my protectors. They just wanted to come. I don't know why they're there."

"Because you can't handle things on your own, I guess," Cass said, scarcely able to believe the words coming out of her.

Ellis's face looked stricken.

Degan's hand was on her arm, telling her to stop.

Ellis said, "I don't need any protectors." He waved at the boys. "Go on, get out of here."

The two boys looked confused for a minute. Then they turned and began walking deliberately away, not looking back.

Ellis crossed his arms, still standing in front of Degan and Cass.

"See? I don't need anyone."

"Yes," Cass snapped, indignation and fury suddenly flowing through her. "I can see you're a perfect bully all on your own."

Strange expressions shot across Ellis's face. Surprise, shock even. Defiance. Misery. Confusion.

"I'm not a bully!"

Then the bell rang.

chapter twelve

Ellis could not keep still, with an energy that was almost frantic. His fingers nimbly constructed small buildings out of marker caps, erasers, tiny ends of pencils that had been chewed to nothing, and stolen sticky tack. They had gables, second stories, porches, shutters. When he was satisfied with them, he knocked them over while making explosion noises, or he fashioned battering rams made from the remains of a broken pencil sharpener and paper clips, and bashed them to pieces.

He kept flicking glances at Cass and Degan, who were passing wadded-up notes back and forth when Ms. Clemens wasn't looking.

Degan wrote, "We can find the mask."

"How?"

"Where did the dream start?"

"My house."

"You should try to remember it."

So Cass sat with her head on her hand, half-closing her eyes, letting her mind drift back to the dream of the night before. At first, all she could think about was that she couldn't empty her mind at all. It was too full of the classroom with shifting students, Ms. Clemens's voice, the movement of the clock. There was too much Ellis sulking in his chair, being angry or hurt or whatever.

But as she grew still, things slowed down.

That sky. Those stars.

Fleeting images shot across her eyes. The stars had almost pulsed, hadn't they?

"I went past the school," she said suddenly.

"I went past the school," Ellis said in a high voice, glaring at the house he was ripping into tiny parts. It was clear he wanted an argument.

Ignoring him, Degan said to Cass: "Then what?"

"I don't know. The stars came after that."

She tried to picture them, floating around her, blinking on and off.

"You two," said Ellis in a low voice, "are crazy."

The annoyance grew in Cass again, a surge made of things the mask sang about that she could scarcely hear but could feel.

"Well, you're racist," she said. Then her eyes opened wide. She could not believe she had said it. Something angry in the mask was encouraging her, and she could hardly help herself.

"No, I'm not!"

"Cass," Degan said softly. "It's all right."

"You are so. You told Degan not to scalp you, and you said something about taxes that I think was supposed to be mean, and you called him an Indian."

"He is an Indian," Ellis said. He frowned. "That's not racist. Everyone talks that way. Besides, it's just a joke."

"I haven't heard anyone else talk that way. Just you."

"Is everything all right?"

Ms. Clemens had walked across the room to them and was now standing over the table.

"It's fine." Ellis sat back in his chair, crossing his arms and slouching down.

"Cass? Degan?"

They nodded.

"How's your work coming along?"

ℭℛ

It felt like forever till the end of the day. The clock seemed to slow down while Ellis sat in offended silence, twisting the sticky tack into little animals and people and then ripping them apart methodically. Meanwhile, Degan and Cass fashioned their plan.

When the bell finally rang, they waited until everyone else had walked out of the class. They put on their coats slowly so that they would be the last to leave the school.

"There he is," Cass whispered.

Ellis was standing on the pavement, looking around, waiting for them.

They waited up against the wall inside the door. Ellis stood there a long time, by himself. Finally, slowly, he began to walk home. He looked surprisingly small.

When he was out of sight, they slipped out the doors and crossed the pavement until they reached the sidewalk.

"This is sort of insane," Cass said, peering around at the perfectly ordinary houses and trees. Along the street in one direction was her home. In the other direction lay an area with shops. Neither direction had any stars at all.

"You were walking away from your house," Degan said calmly. "So…"

He gestured toward the shopping area.

"But it was a place with stars all around, blinking on and off."

He looked at her from under that dark fringe of hair, eyes calm. "Just keep an open mind. And if it turns out this doesn't lead anywhere, what have you lost—besides your mask?"

She took a deep breath.

"Okay. Let's go that way."

They passed a pizza place, a convenience store, a secondhand shop. They walked slowly, looking everywhere for something that might resemble stars. But everywhere were ordinary shop windows, ordinary people going in and out of doors, carrying bags.

Cass said, "I think this is a mistake—" She stopped, and caught her breath.

Ahead of them a neon sign blinked on and off, some of the bulbs burnt out, but enough still glowing. Animated stars seemed to spin around with a jerky motion. Cass could scarcely breathe as she read the words: *STARLIGHT DINER. Our food is stellar!*

chapter thirteen

Cass stared at the sign. It was rusted, practically falling apart. There were certainly stars surrounding the flashing words, but they were flimsy ones that were partially burnt out.

Surely a shabby restaurant sign could not also be a signpost in a dream?

She stared up and down the street of shops, suddenly seeing everything in a new way. Could ordinary, mundane things also be something else?

"Is this it?" Degan asked softly.

She stared up at those blinking lights, that rusted and shabby billboard.

"Yes. Maybe. At least, I think so."

Degan squeezed her arm, his eyes dancing. "You see? This is working!"

She grinned back, catching his excitement.

Now, what had come next in the dream? Would she find that too?

Cass half-closed her eyes. Something about red rock. She remembered darkness, feeling her way through.

"I think we need to look for something red," she whispered to Degan.

It didn't take long to locate the hardware store, made of brownish-red brick. It was next to a barbershop of the same kind of brick. In between the two buildings was a wooden wall connecting them, decorated with posters and advertisements. Inside the barbershop people waited for their haircuts, reading magazines and checking their phones and looking perfectly ordinary. As if the most incredible thing wasn't happening to Cass. As if she wasn't beginning to see how something could be ordinary and part of a dream place at the same time.

"I went through…red rock," she said, remembering. "I…think it was a tunnel. It was dark. I didn't know what was coming."

"Come on." Degan led the way across the road, till they were in front of the red brick hardware store. He walked along the front of the store, running his hand across the brick, looking for a place where a tunnel might be disguised.

Cass hurried to the barbershop and walked closely in front of it too. The people inside looked out at her curiously. A little boy put his hand on the window from the inside. Cass matched her hand with his. He smiled at her, and she smiled back. Everything felt so hopeful all at once.

"I don't see any tunnel," Degan said, coming up beside her. "Maybe there are some other red buildings."

But as they looked up and down the street, they could see only the gray of cement and glass windows.

"Maybe that star sign was just a coincidence," Cass said softly.

Just then, part of the wooden wall between the two buildings opened inward. A woman emerged, walking a dog. She closed the door behind her, turned right, and clicked away.

Cass and Degan stared at each other.

Cass waited till the woman had gone far enough. Then she walked over to the wall. When she was close enough, she could see the hinges. She hesitated, then pushed gently on it.

The door swung inward to reveal an alleyway. It was flanked on both sides by the red brick of the hardware store and the barbershop. The sun could not penetrate it, and so it was dark. Litter scuttled across the alley. A stray cat washed itself on a doorsill.

"Is this it?" Degan asked.

"I—don't know," she said doubtfully.

She stepped into the alley. Somewhere deep in her mind something stirred, a faraway cry.

Suddenly Cass felt half in one world and half in the other. She led the way silently, as if it was a place where it would be wrong to make any noises. There was just the sound of their footsteps. The traffic noises behind them died away, and new sounds began to be heard from what lay ahead.

What *did* lie ahead, anyway? Cass tried to remember the next part of her dream. When she concentrated, an image swam into her mind of something that had been massive, and writhing somehow, curling around.

A snake.

She gulped, and slowed to a stop.

"What is it?" Degan whispered.

"There was a snake next. I went by a gigantic snake."

Degan let out a slow breath. They stared at each other as the magnitude of it sank in.

They had no way of protecting themselves.

Mom didn't even know where Cass was.

Then that faraway sound inside Cass thrummed, like a cat's comforting purr. It seemed to sing that Cass hadn't died in her dream after all, not even when the snake appeared. The mask didn't intend to put her in harm's way. It wanted to be found, that was all. To be with Cass again. It wanted to tell her about things— about how Cass was not the first to be afraid, not alone in being bullied at school.

She took a deep breath, and suddenly she knew she was brave enough to go on, to face whatever was coming. Ignoring the trembling in her legs, Cass started moving forward again. Degan walked beside her.

Then she heard it: a low roaring sound that practically shook the ground underfoot. It grew louder as Cass approached the end of the alleyway—as she drew closer to whatever monster lay ahead.

Did snakes roar?

But the mask was still thrumming reassuringly inside Cass. Its thin faraway sound was somehow stronger in her head than that roaring noise. She took a deep breath and plunged out the end of the alley into whatever might come next.

Flashing, bright colors raced by her at a great speed, blowing Cass's hair back. There was a whir of blurred images, windows blinking one by one, people's faces seen for only a moment before they were gone. The noise was deafening as it hurtled past.

Cass fell back against Degan, who stumbled and fell. They landed in a heap as the thing shot past them, then sat up and watched it go.

Then it dawned on her.

"A train!" she shouted above the din. "The snake is a train!"

Then they were laughing at the top of their lungs, scarcely able to hear each other over the roar of the engine. As quickly as it was there, the train was gone. Then their laughter was much too loud—which made them laugh harder, with relief as much as anything else.

Cass stood up, panting and wiping her eyes.

She grinned at Degan, who was smiling back. It transformed his whole face, and he was suddenly entirely different from the boy she had first met in Ms. Clemens's class, the boy who had sat with his head in his hand and eyes half-closed, sketching and tuning everyone out. Could it really be only yesterday? Somehow it felt like she had known him much longer.

"You're okay," Degan said.

"You're okay too."

And she flushed, because no kid had ever told her that before, ever.

"So where next?" Degan asked at last.

She straightened, closed her eyes. She had followed the curve of the snake to—somewhere.

Then, slowly, she remembered an empty, unhappy place. There had been a kind of mist all around, and even the fiery line of the mask's song had struggled to be seen. Strange shapes had been moving in the fog. She hadn't been able to see them exactly, but she had felt their presence.

Cass shivered involuntarily, as if that fog was trying to get inside her.

"We have to follow the curve of the snake," she said slowly. "I think…it's going to lead us into a place that isn't very happy."

Degan nodded, not questioning for a moment. "Okay."

They walked slowly alongside the fence that separated them from the railway tracks. It curved around, through an area with big cement buildings where the wind whistled, almost like a canyon in the city. They passed a factory with a smokestack. Soon there was nothing but industrial buildings. Still the tracks went on. They curved again, and went down a small slope.

A few scattered houses emerged, small and narrow, with peeling paint. They felt lonely and neglected,

Cass thought. More houses appeared, finally becoming a neighborhood. But unlike Cass's own area of town, where her tough little house was the only one that was not enormous, this whole area was clearly not so well-off. Some of the houses practically backed right up onto the tracks, some of their backyards a jumble of abandoned and rusting things. They were small, narrow, with bending fences and laundry blowing on clotheslines. There were trailers parked on grass. Garbage was strewn in the streets.

"This is it," Cass said softly. "This is the place in the fog. It's the unhappy place."

Degan let out his breath slowly, as if he was going to say something. But then he didn't. Instead, he shoved his hands in his pockets and walked beside her without speaking. She looked sideways at him, sensing the change in his mood. She couldn't see his face because he was looking down at the ground, his hair hanging forward.

"What is it?"

"I live here," Degan said.

chapter fourteen

"Oh!" Cass sucked in air so abruptly that her breath made a noise.

Suddenly she remembered Ellis laughing at where Degan's home was. Hadn't he said something about criminals being there?

"You're right, I guess. It's not a very happy place," he said at last. "As a *place*, that is. There are some good people here, though. Like my aunt."

"And you," Cass said quickly.

She didn't know what to say after that. So they walked silently past the shabby houses, past kids playing on the sidewalks. They were laughing, running around. Kids could make fun anywhere.

Degan said quietly, "My aunt lives here because she says this is where our people need help the most. This is where we've become sick, some of us. Forgetting our roots, lost in the city. So she does healing." After a minute, he added, "She helped my mom, before she died. And she helped me too, when I was a baby. She helped hide me so I wouldn't get taken and put into the foster system."

"My mom was in the foster system," Cass said softly.

Degan glanced at her. He nodded.

They reached some streets with stores on them. Along the narrow streets here, a few people stood around together in doorways or on the sidewalk curbs. They didn't exactly seem to be waiting, but they also didn't seem to have anything to do. Some talked and laughed.

"Degan!"

It was a young man, smoking. He waved. "You learn lots of stuff today?"

Degan nodded and waved back.

"You going to become a professor maybe?"

"Maybe," Degan said.

The young man laughed, not unkindly, and other people laughed too.

It made Cass feel suddenly heavy inside, as if she

was absorbing the atmosphere around her. There was an air of boredom all around, but also, maybe, something else. Something that hung over everyone and whispered about how there was no point in trying to do anything. Nothing would come to anything. Like life itself was a bully, and it was hard to get the energy to keep trying to fight back.

One of the men called to Cass, "You lost, honey?"

She shook her head, eyes down.

"You sure?"

Cass walked faster, while the men behind her laughed. Degan hurried up to walk beside her. They went on without talking for awhile.

Degan finally broke the silence. "Some people around here, they don't have jobs. Maybe they didn't finish high school, and they can't find any work. There's a lot of...sickness."

"What kind of sickness?"

Degan was quiet for a long time again. "Mostly the kind you give to yourself," he said at last. "And some you maybe pick up from other people. Maybe people like Ellis, who tell you you're not worth anything and then say they're joking."

Cass was puzzled about the first part. "How do you give yourself sickness?"

Degan regarded her steadily. "You put things into you that aren't good for you, even though they make you feel better for a little while—that's what my aunt says. Your own thoughts can be sick too. My aunt says some of us have forgotten who we are. We have to heal in our minds and our spirits before we can change anything else around us."

It was Cass's turn to walk silently. She didn't know what to say.

"I live down that street," Degan said, pointing. "But we're going to keep going right now, because we're not done yet. What comes next in your dream?"

She thought hard. It burst into her mind, suddenly glorious.

"I—I climbed into the stars. Up into the sky."

They both looked up at the scudding clouds overhead, as if a stairway might reveal itself. But only birds flew overhead.

Past the little houses, they met up again with the railway tracks. They followed the tracks farther, while the blank backs of big stores began to grow around them, and more cars began to shoot by on the increasingly busy roads.

The sidewalk petered away to nothing but weeds and ruts of mud here and there. They kept walking on the dirt, while the weeds grew longer and more awkward to push through.

At last Cass said, "I don't think this is right."

So they walked between two of the big stores until they reached the large parking lot on the other side. Then they picked through hundreds of parked cars until they were on the sidewalk by the busy road. Several lanes of traffic shot by.

"What do you think?" Degan asked, looking at her again with respect. Like her opinion was to be taken seriously. And he was standing by her, loyal, while she made the decision.

"I think"—she looked at the cars whizzing by—"I think we walk this way."

She took off to the right, and Degan hurried beside her.

Sometime later, the road climbed upward to accommodate another road running beneath. Cass and Degan kept walking along it, while the road sloped upward.

Inside, Cass was listening for the mask. It had been calling her thinly, but now other voices had joined it, and even the materials around her—the cement, the tar, the metal of the cars—seemed to be resonating in her mind somehow. The sounds were building, as if what she needed to notice was nearby.

She looked around. There was nothing but cars, racing by at a great speed, blurs of color and light.

Color and light.

Headlights.

She stopped, grabbed Degan's arm, as she realized the truth. "The stars! The headlights are the stars!"

She pointed to the cars. Here, at the top of the overpass, headlights shot by all around. It was what her dream had intended, she was sure.

"We're getting close," she said, calm coming over her. "We're nearly there."

They walked down the other side of the overpass and into another area with stores. Cass walked ahead carefully, listening for any changes in the sound, confident they would lead her now. The mask was very nearby.

"We turn here."

Degan didn't even question her.

They soon came upon a building with a wide front porch and an arched doorway. Painted above the doorway were pictures of animals—a wolf, a deer, a turtle, some kind of bird, and others. Words were also painted there: *Turtle Island Healing Center.*

An aroma wafted out of the open front doors, where people were walking in and out. Cass suddenly remembered that she had passed a place of plenty and abundance in her dream, with sweet smells.

"Is it a restaurant?" Cass said.

"Nope. It helps people." Degan spoke respectfully. "They do classes, how to find jobs, how to raise your kids, how to get over bad stuff. They have open dinners too. You can go there for a meal. My aunt does some healing circle work with them."

The music was building in Cass now, insistent, pounding.

"It's close. Turn here."

They turned the corner and came upon the store with the large glass window and the sign that read *Ray's Pawnshop*.

chapter fifteen

It was like a dream, but it was really happening. The mask was really here, really inside the pawnshop, Cass was sure of it.

In a daze, she turned the knob and pulled open the glass door. It jingled, a fact that barely registered in her mind. Her regular senses felt dulled, and other phantom senses inside her seemed to be engaging instead.

She and Degan stepped through the doorway.

The man behind the counter was looking at his phone. He had long hair and a beard and was leaning back in his chair. He sat upright when he saw them. He looked them up and down, his eyes lingering on Degan a bit longer than on Cass. As if there was something a little untrustworthy about Degan.

"Hey, kids," he said. "Looking for something?"

"Just browsing," Degan said. His face had taken on that neutral expression it had worn when Cass first met him. Closed suddenly.

"Backpacks up here," the man said.

Cass and Degan put their backpacks on the counter.

"You got money, son?"

"Uh-huh," Degan said.

"Show me."

Degan pulled out some coins and a battered bill from his pocket.

"Okay," said the man, waving them on.

They turned down the first aisle, and the singing inside Cass grew stronger and warmer. Like an animal following a scent, she lifted her head to hear it better.

Turn here, the singers called.

And here.

She was only dimly aware of Degan following her. The mask was just ahead, just around the next aisle.

She took a breath and walked around the last set of shelves. She closed her eyes, willing it to be there.

She opened her eyes.

The music burst in her head, for the mask was hanging there on the wall.

Cass gave a little cry and jumped forward. She couldn't stop herself. She ran her hands down that hair, along the line of the chin. The eyes didn't scare her now, nor did the distorted, half-smiling mouth.

"Here you are," she whispered. "Here you are."

She couldn't have said how long she was caught in that electric reunion. It could have been seconds or hours. But she was startled awake when Degan touched her shoulder gently.

"I have six dollars and forty-three cents," he said. "Do you have anything?"

She shook her head to get the dizziness out. Then she felt inside her pockets, although she already knew the answer.

"No."

"Let's find out how much money we need." Degan's calm voice helped to fix her to the earth again.

Cass followed him to the counter. She realized that she had never thought about needing money. Somehow she had assumed that the mask would simply be coming home with her. But now she saw that the man would never release the mask that easily.

Degan stood awkwardly before the counter.

The man looked up from his phone. "Can I help you?"

Degan said in a clear voice: "The mask. In aisle four. How much is it?" His face twitched slightly, but he maintained a neutral expression.

"The Indian mask?"

Degan nodded his head slightly.

The man grinned. "What do you think it's worth?"

Degan looked down at his feet and thought for awhile. Finally, he looked up again. "I have six dollars and forty-three cents."

The man laughed. "Is that what you think it's worth?"

Degan looked back at him. He shook his head at last.

"How much do you think it's worth?"

Degan whispered, "I don't know."

Cass wanted to shout, *It's worth more than any of us could ever afford. It's worth so much that you can't even measure it in money. It's worth the sky and the earth and birds wheeling overhead.*

But she simply stood quietly and waited beside Degan.

The man said at last, "Thirty bucks. If you have thirty bucks, I'll sell it to you."

Cass's insides fell.

He might as well have said thirty million dollars. She and Mom didn't have thirty dollars to spare. Cass couldn't even imagine having thirty dollars.

"Could—could I work for you?" she asked in a small voice.

"Work for me?" said the man, grinning.

"I could—run errands, clean the shelves, put out garbage. Could I pay for the mask that way?"

Even in her own ears, it sounded feeble.

"It doesn't work like that. I don't employ kids. I sell things, and people pay for them." He glanced down at his phone again. "Are you kids buying something today or not?"

They looked at each other.

"Could you—could you hold it for us?" Cass whispered.

The man shook his head. "If someone comes in five minutes from now, and they have thirty bucks to spare, I'll sell it to them. Because this is a business."

Degan took a deep breath. He nodded to the man, face completely impassive. "Thank you. We'll be back very soon with the money."

"Good to hear," said the man, turning back to his phone.

CR

A minute later, they stood on the sidewalk as the sky began to darken.

Inside Cass, a storm cloud was building, billowing upward. She felt locked up like the mask, separated from her family. Tears were pressing on the backs of her eyes, but she couldn't tell if she was unhappy or furious.

"I will never have thirty dollars," she said dully.

Degan's voice was urgent. "We'll find it. We'll make money. I promise, we'll come up with something. Don't worry."

Then she found that his arm was on her shoulder, and he was propelling her gently forward.

"I'll take you home. It's not far from here, just down King Street. The mask took us in a big loop. And tomorrow we'll figure out how to make money. We'll come back and we'll buy the mask."

She let him lead her on.

She didn't notice the figure moving in the shadows across the street, the one watching her go.

chapter sixteen

"See you tomorrow." Degan lifted a hand, then turned and blended into the darkness. Cass waved back, forcing a smile. But the tightness was still building in her. If the pressure got unbearable enough, what would happen?

She could still hear the mask singing with all of the voices of past and present, like a pulse behind her ears. Angry tears stung her eyes—the mask knew her, and she knew the mask. But it was not hers.

Cass wanted to yell, to kick something.

Instead she took a deep breath and walked slowly up the dirt driveway.

Inside, Mom was sitting at the kitchen table, hunched forward and peering at the computer screen. When Cass opened the door, she jumped up and hugged her. "Where have you been, my darling?"

"I met a friend," Cass said. "Degan."

Mom's eyes lit up with surprise and delight.

"Really?"

Cass nodded. She looked down at her feet. "We— we went for a walk. Just around." She couldn't tell Mom they'd gone looking for the mask. She couldn't bear to see the guilty and sad look on Mom's face again.

She tried changing the subject. "How did it go today? Did you give out your résumés? Did you get any interviews?"

The sunshine faded out of Mom's face, although she smiled brightly. She sat down at the computer again.

"Yes, I gave them all out."

"And?"

She looked up at Cass, tried to smile again. "Well, it's no big surprise. They all said I need to finish high school and get my diploma. At the very least. Most of them said they wanted a university degree. Which is kind of like saying I need to climb Mount Everest."

Cass sat down beside Mom in the silence that followed.

"Well, couldn't you go back to school and get your diploma?"

Mom laughed, but not in a particularly jovial way. The sound was jarring. The mask's song in Cass's head stirred slightly, like ripples created by an object thrown into water.

"Hmm," said Mom in an unfamiliar voice, shoulders hunched and head down. "Yeah, I could do that, my love. I could go back to school, as long as we don't want me to make any money." She let out a shuddering breath.

Cass's insides quivered. Mom wasn't supposed to sound like that.

"The trouble with me," said Mom, "is that I didn't finish high school when I could have. I had the chance, but I didn't take it. And now it's too late. You get caught in a cycle. You need money, so you find a job. But then you're unable to better yourself because you're working all the time."

She sounded so flat, so matter-of-fact.

"What—what about night school?" Cass said tentatively.

Mom laughed again, without humor.

"I can't leave you alone all night."

"Yes, you can."

"No," said Mom. "I can't. My job is to be your mom, to be responsible for you." She looked up at Cass now. "That was the promise I made to you when you were first born, my love. For sure, I wasn't old enough to be having a baby, I wasn't even halfway through high school. But I was determined that I wasn't going to abandon you like my mom did to me. I was going to do everything I could to raise you as well as I could."

Something was starting to build inside Cass. Something dark and angry, all mixed up with the voices in the mask.

"The system," said Mom quietly, "is against me. I did that to myself, though. So tomorrow I'll get something. Washing dishes or cleaning."

She pushed the chair back, stood up, and began to rummage in the cupboards in preparation for dinner.

Cass was tingling all over with electricity that she couldn't control. Everything was building in her to the point of explosion.

Suddenly angry words gushed out of her.

"I'm the reason why you didn't finish high school. That's what you're saying. I stopped you from having a good life."

Mom was staring at her in shock.

"If you'd never had me," Cass said in a cold, shaking,

furious voice, "it would have been better for you. I ruined everything."

She hated the words, hated hearing them, hated saying them, hated how Mom's face turned pink and white and started quivering. But she couldn't help it. The mask's music had somehow turned deadly and dangerous, full of rage.

"No, Cass—"

"You wish I was never born," Cass heard herself saying.

Mom gasped.

Then Cass couldn't bear it anymore. She had to get away, had to escape to a place where she had never said those things to her own beloved mom.

She turned and wrenched open the kitchen door, rushed out into the dark night. The gate was open to the backyard, so she plunged through and ran through the grasses, down the hill to the little stream with the garbage beyond.

She flung herself onto the ground and sobbed. The angry music of the mask crashed not only in her ears, but in the night sounds all around her. It resonated in the rocks, the trees, the grass, the stream. The whole world was filled with rage and regret.

Some time later, hands were on her shoulders and

Mom's head was against her head. Then Mom had Cass in her arms, and she was rocking her slowly while Cass's sobs shook her whole body.

Mom rocked her forever, until finally Cass's breath began to slow into long, shuddering breaths. Mom's arms held Cass stronger than anything, like great roots wrapped all around.

"Shhh," Mom kept saying. "Shhh."

Slowly the music inside Cass and all around in the night began to subside too. The jarring, rage-filled sounds transformed into something else.

Cass whispered at last: "I'm sorry."

Mom squeezed her tighter. She whispered back, "You are the one good thing that has ever happened to me. You are everything—my one, my girl, my darling. We are—we are each other's roots."

Cass thought about that as they sat side by side on the hill, leaning together for warmth and comfort. She and Mom, they were like a tree that barely knew which way to grow. It was feeling its way through rocky ground, struggling to dig roots down, and reaching blindly up for sunlight. It hadn't given up, for some weird reason, although it should have.

Yes, the mask and the night world seemed to sing. *Struggling, surviving, even when you don't think you can, that is the story of life on this planet. Your lonely fight is not really lonely at all, when you think that everyone else is fighting too.*

Mom said softly, "Listen to the night. Listen. So many different sounds, like different stories."

Cass whispered, "Like music."

Mom held her close. "Like music."

chapter seventeen

Mom hugged her and hugged her, and tucked the blankets all around her chin, just as she had when Cass was little. Then she kissed her on the forehead. "Good night, my darling."

After Mom had closed the door, Cass lay in bed thinking. What would it have been like for Mom, for Cass, if Mom had not become a foster child? Would Mom have had the confidence to finish high school, or to even go to university? And would Cass have been there at all?

She thought, as she had several times, of the crumpled envelope. After rescuing it from the garbage, she had put it in her pocket. Later she had placed it in the dresser, in the empty drawer where the mask had been. Since then, she had opened the drawer to look at it, but that was all.

Cass's mind churned around that envelope and whatever secrets it might hold. What did it say?

She pushed the covers back and slipped out of bed, pulled out the drawer softly. Cass lifted the smoothed-out envelope in her hands, staring at it.

Should she?

But if she learned something, something important, how could she ever tell Mom about it?

And could she live with knowing something important, but not sharing it?

The mask might be far off, in Ray's Pawnshop. But it was still quietly thrumming, as if letting her work it out. It was like a heartbeat in the background, encouraging but not directing her. Like she had to figure out what to do herself.

Cass wanted badly to open it. She wanted to know. She wanted Mom to know.

She sat a long time on the edge of the bed, holding the envelope. It was right here, everything, she was sure.

But in the end, she placed the envelope back in the drawer and slid it shut.

Not right now, she thought. *Maybe never, or maybe someday.*

She drifted down into another dream.

❦

The mask was calling her again, intertwined voices like vines of fire, drawing her out of her bed. Again, the wall was like mist. Cass floated through.

The voices led her through the gate. Then Cass was floating along the grass, down the hill toward the river and into the dumping ground beyond. The voices began to swirl around each other, like a tornado. As they swirled, they grew ever higher.

And in their midst, something green and determined thrust itself up through the garbage and began to grow.

It was tiny at first, a seedling. But as it grew, Cass could see it was a white pine tree. Stronger and taller it stretched, as the voices spun around it.

Then Cass felt herself rising, beginning to swirl around the tree too. She rose dizzyingly, ever higher. The earth fell away beneath her, and she was amid the stars. She could see everything, like an eagle.

There were lakes there, stretching out like fingers. And around the lakes, winking lights looked like little fires.

People were grouped around them, families. Thin spires of smoke spiraled upward from the fires, carrying prayers toward the sky that seemed so fragile that they might blow away on the wind.

Something was familiar. Something in the glint of starlight on the waters, reflecting Cass back at herself.

Suddenly it came to her.

This was the lake! The one she would float upon when bullies were too much and she needed to escape. It was the one from her daydream, where she drifted with the movement of the water.

A fireball exploded below.

It spread out across the quiet land, bathing it in flames. The people cried out, their voices mingling with the tortured singing of the mask.

Cass could hear her own voice crying "No!"

The people were running now, trying to escape. They scattered, and the families were all separated. They rushed blindly in all directions.

But they couldn't escape, for the fire organized itself and it became lines of brutal flames, a grid that came down over the land. It held the people in as if it were the window of a jail, and they could barely move.

The children still reached for the sky, where Cass was watching in horror. But the flames separated them from

126

everyone else, drew them together like bewildered cattle, put them in their own jail.

With a shock, Cass realized: the jail was that building. The dark one from her earlier dream, with the bell tower and bars on the windows.

The children had been rounded up like animals, corralled in by the lines of fire, and they had no hope of escape.

Then the mask's voices rose in grief. Their cries cast across the sky, seeking justice. They were no match for that cruel fire. Not yet. So all they could do was sob with the unfairness of it.

Cass sobbed too.

ༀ

When she awoke, her cheeks were wet with real tears and she was gasping for breath. She sat up, blinked at the sunshine coming in through the windows.

It was all right, she told herself. Cass was safe and Mom was safe. It had just been a bad dream.

But it lingered with her as she got dressed. That fire. Those children.

Why did she keep dreaming of the children?

Mom was making oatmeal in the kitchen, and the smell of coffee hung in the air. Cass hugged her from behind, because it was all so warm. She and Mom, they were really managing. And everything would be okay.

When they sat down to eat together, Mom said, "I've been thinking about what you said. About going back to school. You are such a wise kid."

Cass took a spoonful of oatmeal and waited.

"Should I…talk to Mr. Gregor about it?" Mom asked.

"About going back to school?"

"All of it," Mom said, her voice slow. "Is it possible for me to work and look after you if I go back to school? Maybe he has advice about jobs, what courses I'd need to take if I went past school into—well—college or something." She laughed. "It sounds pretty stupid when I say it out loud. And I don't even know how much he'd be willing to help. I don't really like to ask for help, anyway."

She sounded like she was trying to talk herself out of it.

"I might not be able to do it. I'm pretty dumb, really."

Cass heard her voice exploding in the same moment as the mask's voices exploded inside her. "You are not dumb! And yes, I think you should talk to Mr. Gregor. He already said he wants to help!"

The images from her dream were so fresh, so stark in her head. It was as if Mom was caught in that grid and couldn't get out.

chapter eighteen

Degan was beside the tree again, leaning against it, arms crossed, when Cass left for school. It had been only a day since she had last seen him, since they had made that extraordinary, magical journey to find the mask. Yet so much had happened with Cass and Mom, that time seemed all mixed up.

"I have an idea," he said, looking up as she walked down the driveway.

"Good morning to you too."

"Good morning." He flashed a brief grin at her, then got back to business. "So, I think I've figured out how we can make money to buy the mask. Wanna hear?"

Cass glanced up at the big houses they were passing, where people probably had all the money in the world. What would it be like to live in one of them, to be one of those people? They could buy the mask in an instant.

"Sure."

"Well, you actually gave me the idea. You said I could be an artist one day." Degan's eyes were dancing. "What if we go to the mall after school, and I put up a sign saying I'll sketch people's portraits for five dollars?"

Cass frowned, not sure why. "I can't take your money."

"It wouldn't be mine. It would be ours."

"You'd be doing their portraits. It'd be your money."

Degan let out a long breath. "You'd be, you know, collecting the money, talking to people, drumming up business."

Cass shook her head and kept walking.

"Well, why not?" Degan said, sounding like he was trying not to be exasperated. "Why can't you let me try to help you? What's wrong with letting people help you?"

The words made Cass stop.

It was almost exactly what she had just said to Mom.

If Mom was caught in that grid from Cass's dream, was Cass caught in it too?

"I...don't know," she said slowly.

"Exactly," said Degan. "So let me help."

CR

During class, Degan worked on some practice sketches that he would use to advertise for business when they got to the mall. He drew Cass while she worked and exactly captured her expression, even down to how frustrated she felt trying to complete the assignment their teacher had just explained. He also sketched Ms. Clemens and did a wide view of the whole classroom, providing a perfect likeness of students writing, staring out the window, playing with items in their desks, or chatting with each other.

Meanwhile, Ellis was building a miniature golf course on his desk. He fashioned obstacles and various towers with moving parts. There were embankments and cunning turns the ball had to make in order to reach the targets. When Ms. Clemens came by, he held his open binder above it, so it looked like he was working. The golf course occupied most of his attention, although Cass caught him sneaking urgent glances at her as if he had something he really wanted to say but couldn't figure out how to do it.

At least he is quiet for once, Cass thought.

After school, they waited again while Ellis trudged off. Then Degan said, "I have to stop by my house to get my good art supplies."

"Okay."

They walked toward King Street, taking a direct route today, instead of the roundabout journey the mask had taken them on yesterday. They passed the houses in need of paint and repair, and turned onto Degan's street.

He stopped in front of a small two-story house. At the side of it was a metal fire-escape staircase. "We go up here. We live upstairs, my aunt and I."

Cass followed Degan up the staircase, trying to ignore that it was shaking slightly. She convinced herself not to look down at the ground below.

Degan practically ran up the stairs, not bothered at all by the height. At the top, he wiped his feet on the mat, knocked lightly, and opened the door. Then he walked through and gestured for Cass to follow him.

Cass stepped into a little hallway with yellow wall-paper, where shoes were neatly lined up. She removed her shoes and lined them up too.

A voice called, "Deganawida?"

"Yes, Kehji. It's me."

"Sge:no, baby."

"I want to introduce you to someone, Kehji," Degan said.

He gestured to Cass to follow him along the hallway and into a living space. Cass's heart beat a bit faster, suddenly shy. Her whole life, it had never been a very good thing meeting new people. She gulped and glanced back at the door, half-wondering if she should make an excuse and leave.

But a woman with flowing black hair stepped into the hallway, smiling.

"This is Cass," Degan said. "The one I told you about."

He turned to Cass. "This is my aunt."

Degan's aunt smiled down at Cass, eyes crinkling with welcome. They held a kindness that seemed to go on forever. She took Cass's hands. "I've heard so much about you. You're the one who hears the Orenda, yes?"

Cass blinked, utterly startled by Degan's aunt's calm words.

"Hears the wh—what?"

Was that her mask's name? Orenda?

Could Degan's aunt help to explain what was going on?

Her shyness forgotten, she stared into the lady's kind

face with its limitless calm. She said, "Why do I hear it? Why me?"

"I'm going to make us tea," Degan's aunt said.

Degan protested, "We only have a little while. We're going to the mall. I'm going to make sketches, and we're going to earn money to buy back the false face I told you about."

"All the more reason," Degan's aunt said very calmly, "to have a small talk first. She should know what she's getting into. Those things are slippery."

She disappeared out of the room, and Cass could hear clinking cups, a kettle being filled.

Degan ran his hands distractedly through his hair. But Cass didn't mind the delay. In fact, her insides were very nearly buzzing with excitement. She suspected that she was about to get answers to a whole lot of questions.

chapter nineteen

"So—how did a kid such as yourself get a mask like that?"

Degan's aunt poured out tea into chipped mugs and handed them around.

Cass looked into her face. She felt that she could trust her.

"It's a long story."

"Long stories," said Degan's aunt, "are the best kind."

Then the words were suddenly spilling out of Cass. It was the story of everything. She told about Mom growing up in the foster care system. About how when Mom was a teen she had Cass and struggled to raise her baby even though she was little more than a child her-self. Then, about how they had heard the news from Ms. Maracle about Mom's mom. About Mom being so angry about taking anything, but finally deciding to put it all in Cass's name.

She told about Mom taking that letter from Ms. Maracle and throwing it into the garbage at the end of the yard. And about Cass rescuing it. But about how she couldn't open it.

Then Cass described moving into the house, and the strange moment of tracing the music to the drawer, slid-ing it open, and finding the mask. And about how the mask had not left her alone since, whether she was awake or asleep. Even when it had been sold to the pawn-shop, it kept singing. It was always tangling around her thoughts, embedding itself in everything Cass was doing or thinking.

At last she finished, while the music from the mask licked around the sides of her mind like the memory of flames.

She waited anxiously to hear what Degan's aunt would have to say.

"What's it singing about?"

Cass thought hard about that.

"I—I don't know, really," she said at last. "The mask is showing me things. Telling me things. It's in my dreams."

"Tell *me*." Degan's aunt sipped her tea, hands cupped around the mug.

Cass took a deep breath, then she began. As she spoke, the pictures from her dreams rose in her mind as if they were happening all over again.

There was the dark building with bars on the windows. Suddenly Cass was back inside with the children who had been rounded up. Again, she was feeling their terror and confusion. They didn't know why they were there, what they had done wrong.

Next she was remembering that white pine tree. It was growing taller, while the mask's voices encircled it like ropes of living fire. Again, Cass rose high, high into the air, circling around the tree like an eagle, until she could see everything: the winking fires below that sent fragile prayers into the sky, the horrible explosions rolling across the land like lakes of fire, and the grid stretching over the land, ensnaring everyone and rounding the children up like beasts.

She wasn't aware of the tears rolling down her face until Degan handed her a tissue. He patted her shoulder.

"That's a lot to live through," Degan's aunt said

kindly. She clasped Cass's hands, put them together, patted them.

"What does it mean?" Cass whispered.

Degan's aunt kept patting her hands.

"That mask is telling you the story of our people. The Haudenosaunee. The Iroquois. From the beginning, right up to now."

She smiled into Cass's eyes. "We are the people you saw by the lakes, you know. There were five nations that came together in peace, the Iroquois Confederacy. They were the Seneca, Mohawk, Cayuga, Oneida, and Onondaga. Then, later, the Tuscarora. Our symbol is the white pine, with an eagle at the top."

Her eyes grew dark. "Those explosions, that grid of fire that you saw—I can tell you about that too. We were driven from our homes by people who came from other places. White people, Europeans. They killed many of us. They tried to force the rest of us into small pieces of land. Reservations. We weren't allowed to leave. That's how they kept track of us, controlled us."

"Tell her about the schools," Degan said softly. "With the kids."

"They took our children," Degan's aunt said, patting Cass's hands some more. It was strangely comforting, an act of peace, supporting Cass through bad news. "They put them in schools. Those places were called residential schools. They wanted to make the children forget who they were, forget their past. They tortured them, beat them, starved them. Made them ashamed of who they were. Now those children are grown up. They are having a terrible time knowing who they are."

The tears welled up in Cass again, for the mask was singing beautifully alongside Degan's aunt, calling out that her words were true. It was a raw, gorgeous cry.

"Why is it singing to me?"

Degan's aunt smiled. "Why does anything happen? You know how to listen. You're able to hear the Orenda, flowing through that false face, going right back to the beginning of time. Believe me, that's a rare gift."

There was that word again.

"What does it mean—*Orenda*?" Cass asked.

"It's the life force, powerful healing magic. You can direct it to help people. But be careful. It can be channeled for bad things too. Used to hurt. Then we could call it the Otkon."

Suddenly Cass thought of the rage that had built in her yesterday when she couldn't rescue the mask. She had come home and her fury had burst at Mom. The mask had sung right along with her, as angry as she was. She had used her words to hurt Mom.

Had that been the Otkon?

"I can teach you," said Degan's aunt, as if reading her mind. "Teach you about how people channel the Orenda for healing. Help you to know the Otkon and avoid it. Also, if you're going to have that false face around, you could probably use some lessons in how to get along with it. Because they can be ornery things, you know."

Cass nodded, her mind reeling.

"But first," Degan's aunt added gently, "you need to rescue it from the pawnshop. A mask like that should never have been sold and put on display. It's alive. A holy thing. Our people don't believe a false face is a decoration, something to buy to brighten up a wall."

"That's why we have to go." Degan got up. "We need to make the money so we can buy it back."

Cass whispered, "My mom didn't mean to do the wrong thing. She—we needed money, that's all. She didn't know false faces shouldn't be sold. She didn't mean to be disrespectful."

"There's no shame in needing money."

Degan's aunt stood too, with nothing but peace in her eyes. She held out her hands to Cass, who also rose.

"You and Degan, you can go and make this right."

chapter twenty

The mall was busy with predinner shoppers—people who had just gotten off work, school kids hanging around, parents with strollers. Cass was overwhelmed by light and sound as she followed Degan along a broad, bright corridor, past the crowds.

"Do you know where you're going?"

He threw a deadpan glance over his shoulder at her, then kept walking till they reached an open area where several avenues met. There was a fountain in the middle with benches all around.

"I thought we could set up here."

They organized themselves on one of the benches.

Degan set out his sketch pad and pencils. He laid out some of the sketches he had made earlier, so that people walking by could see them. Then Cass stood up, holding the sign Degan had created during class that afternoon.

HAVE YOUR PORTRAIT SKETCHED
Results Guaranteed
$5

She walked around, feeling slightly foolish. For the most part, people passed by, read the sign, and kept walking. A couple laughed.

"Nice shirt," a girl said once.

Cass blushed furiously. Why was she putting herself in front of people who were just going to laugh at her? Had she learned nothing from being bullied for so long?

But then she glanced at Degan, whose hand was scraping across the sketch pad in front of him at rapid speed. His face was tight and intent, and Cass could tell he was capturing the movement, the craziness, the living energy of everything around him.

And he was doing it all for her, just so she could buy back the mask.

A woman with a stroller came by just then. Her face was crimson with all kinds of feelings, Cass thought—tiredness, stress, wanting to get home. Nonetheless, the lady slowed to read the sign and to look at the pictures Degan had placed on the bench.

She stood for a long time staring at them before she spoke. "These are very good! Did you do them all by yourself?"

"Yes, I did." Degan glanced up at her. He kept his face calm, but Cass could feel his pleasure at the lady's words.

"Are you raising money for something?"

"It's"—he glanced at Cass—"it's for a friend. To get something she needs."

Cass flushed again. She wanted to tell Degan to stop. It felt awkward to tell anyone that she needed something. It felt strange and unpleasant to have Degan say out loud that he was helping her.

Then she thought again of Mom. Mom had been so guarded with Mr. Gregor the first few times he came over. She could barely look him in the eye, even though he had offered help in lots of different ways.

Mom didn't want to take aid from anyone. But she had told Cass that morning that she was going to go and ask for Mr. Gregor's help.

If Mom could do it, maybe Cass could.

The mask's voices stirred inside her, spurring her on. "It's for me."

The lady smiled at her. "What do you need to buy with the money?"

Cass gulped, but the voices helped her to stay steady. "My mom pawned something of mine. A mask. We want to try to buy it back."

The lady looked from Degan's face to Cass's, and back again.

"What kind of a mask?"

"An Iroquois false face," Degan said.

The lady nodded. She drew the blanket more closely around the baby in the stroller. "Are you Iroquois?" she asked Degan.

He nodded. "Cayuga Nation."

"What about you?" she asked Cass.

"No," Cass said. "I'm nothing, really."

It was true. Mom didn't know anything about her background, and so Cass didn't either. And it had never struck her until that moment that it was a bit like a hole inside her, not knowing. Like part of Cass wasn't there.

"I wouldn't say you were nothing," said the lady kindly.

Just then, two tall men approached. They wore name tags that said *Mall Security*.

"Hello, kids," said one of them. "How we all doing this afternoon?"

"Fine." Degan's face took on the closed look it had at the pawnshop, when the man asked him if he had any money.

"What are you doing here today? Selling some pictures?"

Degan nodded.

"You've got a permit for that, I'm assuming?"

Degan looked blankly at Cass, who looked helplessly back at him.

"I didn't know we needed one," Degan said.

"Oh yeah, to sell stuff on mall property, you need a permit."

The other man said, "If you don't have a permit, we're going to have to ask you to leave, son."

"How—how do we get a permit?" Cass asked desperately. "We could go get one right now."

"Got to apply to city hall, bunch of paperwork," said the first man. "Doesn't happen just like that. I'm sorry, kids, but we're going to have to ask you to leave."

Degan slowly began to gather his materials, his face still expressionless. The men waited until Degan stood up with everything in his arms. Cass couldn't bear to feel Degan's disappointment. She put a hand on his shoulder.

"It's okay. We'll try somewhere else. It doesn't matter."

The men walked them to the door of the mall and held the door open for them to go through. The lady with the stroller came out behind them.

"Thank you," she said to the security men as they held the door for her.

"No problem, ma'am. Have a nice evening." He closed the door again. Then the security men stood inside and stared at Degan and Cass.

It was starting to rain, on top of everything else. Degan's sketch pad would be ruined. He and Cass stood under the mall's awning, looking out at the falling drops, trying to decide what to do.

The woman with the stroller leaned over beside them, tucking a plastic cover around the stroller. Her voice was so muffled Cass could hardly hear it. "So how much do you need?"

"Pardon?"

The lady straightened. "For the mask. How much is it? Do you know?"

Degan and Cass looked at each other.

"It's thirty dollars," Cass said softly.

The lady smiled. "For thirty dollars, I bet you could do a beautiful portrait of Rose." She stroked her baby's head under the plastic hood.

"Portraits are five dollars," Degan said, his voice steady and tight.

"Make it thirty-five," said the lady. "These guys in pawnshops can raise the price at a moment's notice."

"We don't have anywhere to do it."

The lady gestured along the street. "Look at all the places. Why don't we go into the nearest doughnut shop, and I'll treat you to something while you do Rose's portrait."

Cass whispered, "Why would you do this for us?"

The lady shrugged and smiled. "I think you should have your mask. I'm sorry your mom had to pawn it. I'd like to help you get it back. It sounds like it means a lot to you."

Degan looked at Cass. Then he looked at the lady. "It does."

"Well, then, come on. I'm Eleanor, by the way."

"I'm Cass. He's Degan," Cass said shyly.

chapter twenty-one

The doughnut shop was warm and bright after the gray rain. Eleanor wheeled her stroller up to the counter. She ordered hot chocolate for Cass and Degan, and a tea for herself. She bought everyone a doughnut. Then they all moved to a table in the corner.

A few minutes later, after sipping some hot chocolate, Degan asked, "Can I?"

He gestured to the stroller. Inside, nestled next to baby Rose, was the sketchbook. Eleanor had insisted on putting it in there to keep it dry.

He reached in and gently removed it. Eleanor smoothed the blanket around Rose and ran a finger along her cheek. Rose smiled and gurgled. But then she began to wriggle as her Mom took her hand away. After a minute the little face scrunched together, and she opened her tiny mouth to emit a loud, scratchy squawk.

"Shhh, shhh," said Eleanor. "She's hungry."

She rummaged in a large bag, through diapers and toys. She pulled out a bottle, placed it on the table. Then she lifted out Rose and expertly cradled her in one arm while inserting the bottle into the baby's mouth with the other hand. She rocked her back and forth, and Rose settled into it.

"Want me to draw her like that? You holding her, the bottle."

Degan looked intent, confident. Like everything was in harmony in that moment. Cass suddenly thought of the sketch he had made of the man at the top of the cliff. In this minute, if Degan was that man, he might just stay there—neither jump nor fall. Just be part of everything, completely himself. It was as if that life force, the Orenda, was flowing through him.

If only Mom could feel that way. Or me.

"That sounds nice," said Eleanor.

So Cass watched as the mother fed her baby, and Degan's hand meandered around the page in front of him, his eyes flicking up and down.

Eleanor smiled and tried to hold still. Rose snuggled close. They were in harmony too.

Then, growing out of that ordinary doughnut shop, out of the cement and wood and even plastic around her, she could feel the song of the mask rising. It was like in her dream, when everything felt alive. They knew Cass, knew Degan, Eleanor, and Rose. They were surrounding them with warmth and light and wisdom, even in the midst of a rainy afternoon with people coming and going in muddy boots. Was that the Orenda too?

Was it everywhere? Did you just have to know how to look—and listen?

Eleanor was smiling at Degan, smiling at Rose. *She is happy,* Cass thought. And her happiness had spread like ripples to Degan, because he was happy too, as he sketched. Could harmony inside a person flow to other people around you?

How did you get that harmony? Were you born with it? Could you learn it? Was it easier if your life wasn't made up of bills and the food bank and trying to find work when you hadn't finished high school?

The music inside Cass altered slightly—as if it was a river that had hit a narrow channel, where rocks caused it to gnarl and churn as it went. It was the same river, only it took the shape and character of what was around and under it. It was tortured and wild because the rough river bed had forced it to be that way. Kind of like Mom.

Mom, who worked hard. Mom, who hated help. Mom, who loved Cass beyond anything. Just like this lady loved her baby.

Mom had the same Orenda inside her as Eleanor did. It just looked different. It wasn't flowing calmly because it hadn't had a chance yet. But it was a life force all the same. And maybe Mom could learn to channel it for good things, just as Cass was going to learn to do.

♋

When Degan had finished, Eleanor drew in her breath sharply. "You captured us. It is perfect."

"Thanks," Degan said shyly.

Eleanor placed Rose, who was now asleep, back into the stroller and tucked the blanket around her. Then she pulled out her wallet and removed some bills. "Thirty-five dollars, just as we agreed."

She slid a card toward Degan. "I teach art history at the university. You are a very talented young man. I can probably help you, if you're interested."

Degan's eyes widened.

"Think about it," said Eleanor. To Cass she added, "And at the very least, I would love an opportunity to see that mask of yours sometime, once you get it back. If it's authentic, it is very significant and special."

Cass nodded shyly. "Thank you."

Then, minutes later, they were dashing through the rain, Degan's sketchbook zipped up inside his coat. And it was as if Eleanor had almost been a strange dream—the right person coming along, just when she was most needed. She was a weird coincidence.

Though Cass was starting to wonder if the ordinary world was pretend, and if the real world, the real way things were, was full of coincidences like Eleanor.

೦෪

The man was turning the *OPEN* sign to *CLOSED* when they arrived at the pawnshop.

"Please," Cass said, out of breath. "Can't we please come in? We have money!" She pulled the crumpled bills from her pocket. "And we know just what we want to buy!"

The man sighed and looked at his watch. "One minute."

"Thank you!"

They raced inside, and along to the farthest aisle by the wall.

Then stopped dead.

Where the mask had hung, there was now an empty space.

"Where is it?" Cass said loudly, to nobody in particular. She looked around helplessly, as if the mask might possibly have chosen to move to another place.

The man came, drawn by her voice.

"What are you looking for?"

"The…the mask. It was hanging here, just yesterday. It was thirty dollars. Don't you remember?" Her voice was rising, and her hands were shaking.

"Relax," said the man. "I'm sorry, but it got sold. Pretty popular mask, I've gotta say."

"Sold?" Cass said blankly.

Degan had been standing quietly by, but now he asked: "Do you know who bought it?"

The man shrugged. "A kid. Kind of tall, reddish hair. Big kid. About your age."

chapter twenty-two

The rain was really pouring down now, like the sky could feel what was happening to Cass and Degan.

"He sat there!" Cass shouted. "He sat there today in class and he knew! He knew!"

She was bent over, hands on knees, genuinely dizzy with fury.

"He must have followed us yesterday." Degan stood completely still in the rain, as if he was made of rock.

"And then he bought it! How could he?"

Even with all of her experiences with bullies, Cass had never imagined Ellis might go and buy the mask for himself. But now that the truth was exploding all around her like the rain, it all started to become clear. He had certainly laid the groundwork carefully, stalking them, finding out what they were looking for, learning how much it cost, then buying it before them, either yesterday or today.

The dishonesty, the cruelty of it was more than she could handle. Rain and tears soaked her cheeks.

"Okay. We're going over there." Degan stood straighter and shook his sopping hair out of his eyes.

"Where?"

"Where do you think?" Degan's eyes were flashing. "His house, of course. We're going to go and get it back."

Cass's heart was beating so fast she could hardly breathe. "He won't give it to us," she said, bent over still, trying to get air into her lungs.

"Oh, he'll give it to us." Degan's voice was eerily calm. Almost scary.

Cass looked up. She thought suddenly of Degan's aunt saying that if you weren't careful, you could channel the Orenda for bad things—the Otkon.

"What are you going to do? You can't hurt him."

However much Ellis deserves it, she thought.

"I won't hurt him," Degan said smoothly. "We're going to have a talk. We're going to get to the bottom of this."

156

"Do you know where he lives?"

Degan had already started walking. "He's on your street."

∞

By the time they had reached Cass's street, the sky was darkening even more and evening was approaching. Lights blinked on in the big houses as families gathered together, safe and warm inside. *Rich families,* Cass thought bitterly. Ellis was rich.

Degan turned up a driveway that was running with rainwater. They trudged up against the rivulets. They climbed the rounded staircase to the front porch, where two elegant wicker chairs were set out. The chairs looked like they had never been sat in.

Cass and Degan stared at each other, half-panicked and half-determined.

Degan knocked loudly.

It took a long time for someone's footsteps to approach inside. The outside light switched on, and a man's face appeared in the decorative glass window of the front door. The man frowned, then unlatched the door.

"Yes? Can I help you?"

He was looking them up and down with profound

distrust. Cass realized how unkempt and disheveled they must look, how sodden with rain.

"Is Ellis here?"

"He might be." The man gazed at Degan's long hair and the features of his face. "What do you need him for?"

"He has something," Degan said, "that belongs to us. We want to talk to him about that."

The man frowned. "What is it?"

"A mask," Cass said, finding her voice.

"What, a Halloween mask?"

"An Iroquois mask. A false face." She stood her ground against the condescension in his eyes.

The man began to inch the door closed. "Listen, this isn't a good time, and whatever you want, we're not interested. We're having dinner."

Behind him, Ellis began to walk slowly down the curving staircase. The man followed the direction of Cass's eyes, and turned around to see him.

Ellis was moving cautiously, like a cat. Like he expected to have to run suddenly. In his hand he carried the mask, its hair flowing over his arms.

His father said sharply, "What's that thing? What's it doing in our house?"

Ellis froze, eyes on his father's face.

"You're not putting that piece of garbage in your

the mask that sang

room," his father exploded. "You've got enough in there already. All those stupid doodads you keep making."

Ellis stuck his jaw out, but he stayed quiet.

Cass was suddenly embarrassed to be standing there listening to this. Ellis's face was watchful, as if he expected to be struck.

She knew how that felt.

The last thing she expected was to feel sorry for him. But she did.

"That thing belongs to these kids?" Ellis's father boomed.

Ellis said dully but stubbornly: "I bought it."

"But you knew it was mine," Cass blurted.

"Where did you buy it?" asked the man, ignoring her.

"Pawnshop."

Ellis's father shook his head, disgust on his face. "What were you doing in a pawnshop?"

Ellis shrugged.

Degan stepped forward. "Cass's mother had to pawn it. We were trying to buy it back. Then Ellis went and bought it himself."

"Ohhh," said the man. He put his hands in his pockets and nodded. Then he blinked, a kind of mock confusion on his face. He leaned close to Degan's face. "Pardon me, but are you telling me you've come to our house at this time of night because my son bought something, and you don't like it? Seriously? When do you people get to decide who buys your tribal stuff or whatever?"

He turned to Ellis. "How much was it?"

Face drawn, Ellis muttered, "Thirty bucks."

The man shook his head some more. "Thirty bucks for that piece of garbage?"

Ellis said nothing.

"We want to buy it from him," Degan muttered.

Ellis's father said, "Have you got any money?"

"We have thirty-five dollars."

Ellis's father opened the door slightly. "Come here," he said to Ellis.

Ellis moved forward watchfully, holding the mask tightly as if someone was going to grab it.

His father gazed down at the mask as if it was some dead and rotting thing. He looked at Degan and Cass, dripping with rain.

"Forty," he said.

"We don't have forty!" Cass cried, fury bubbling up.

Ellis's father shrugged. He began to close the door again, this time for good. He turned to Ellis, now out of sight, and said, "Get that thing away from me. Throw it out. It's not staying here."

"If you're throwing it out, why can't we have it for thirty-five dollars?" Degan asked desperately.

Ellis's father looked at him impassively. "If your people spent a little more time developing some business skills and less time drinking and carving this kind of stuff"—he gestured to the mask—"they might be a bit higher on everyone's radar. I don't mean to be unkind. It's just a fact. If you want this mask, you'll do some honest work for it."

He was forcing them back, toward the rain and the night. The last thing Cass saw, as the door slowly closed, was Ellis's stricken face on the stairs.

As if he'd wanted to say something quite different but hadn't had a chance.

chapter twenty-three

Cass could barely hear anything Degan was saying. It wasn't that she was thinking about something else. She just wasn't hearing things right, or seeing them right, or something. She was just walking along in the rain, that was all.

"We'll just get some more money," Degan repeated. "Five more dollars, and we'll buy it back."

Cass looked at him blankly.

"No."

She would not try to get the mask back anymore. She would not negotiate with that man for something that wasn't important to him. It would make her too embarrassed and ashamed to buy anything—but especially something that mattered so much—from someone who had no respect for her.

The Orenda was singing inside her, anyway. It had never stopped. The Orenda would keep bubbling and gushing with life in all things, in all places, whether Ellis had Cass's mask or not.

So she didn't need the mask, not really.

Although her insides were sobbing at its loss.

෴

They had reached her driveway.

"Good night," Cass said dully, and turned to walk up toward the door.

"It'll be okay," Degan said, his voice tight. "Tomorrow we'll make a new plan."

She nodded without agreeing, and turned the knob to enter the kitchen. She closed the door softly behind her, shutting Degan out in the rain.

The kitchen was dark, with only the light over the stove gleaming faintly. At first, Cass could make out very little. Then she realized with a start that Mom was sitting at the kitchen table, her head cradled in her hands.

"Mom?" Cass whispered. "Are you okay?"

Mom looked up. Even in the half-darkness, Cass could see that she had been crying.

"Oh, Mom! What is it?"

Cass tumbled into the chair beside Mom and wrapped her arms around her. Mom sank into Cass's arms, resting her head on Cass's shoulder. Not for the first time, Cass felt responsible for Mom, as if Mom were her child.

Cass tried desperately to imagine what could possibly be wrong. Mom had been planning to speak to Mr. Gregor about how to maybe go back to school. Had she found out that was impossible?

"Did—did you talk to Mr. Gregor? Did something go wrong?"

Surely Mr. Gregor wouldn't have said something unkind?

Mom took a shuddering breath and sat up. She smoothed her hair and wiped under her eyes with the tissue beside her. Then she shook her head the way she did when she wanted to get the unhappiness out, and get on with things. She smiled, suddenly Mom again, though rumpled.

"Oh, yes, I talked to Mr. Gregor." She gave a short, sharp laugh. "That seems like a million years ago."

"What did he say?"

"What did he say?" Mom repeated in a faraway voice. "He actually helped me a lot. I can take some courses online to get my GED—that's my high-school graduation. And he looked at my résumé and said he thought I might be able to do some cooking in his sister's daycare, because she's looking for a cook."

She stared down at her hands like they weren't hers.

"So then he called his sister. And then I went over to the daycare and met her. And she's hired me—on probation for a few weeks, but permanent after that if it works out. I'm starting tomorrow. So I can do that in the day and get my GED at night."

"That's wonderful!" Cass cried.

"And she gave me an advance of money." Mom blinked at Cass, with eyes that seemed to only partly see her. "So, I did what I promised you I'd do. I went over to the pawnshop, where I pawned your mask. You know, the one you liked. I promised I would get it for you when I got a job."

Cass drew her breath in slowly.

Tears filled Mom's eyes again.

"It was sold."

Cass nodded.

Mom whispered, "I let you down, honey. You don't ask for much, but that was something you really wanted.

Mother of the year, here, took it away and then couldn't get it back for you."

"Oh, Mom. No."

"So then," Mom said, "I was sitting here thinking about that mask. And wondering why you felt such a connection to it." Her voice got low. "And I thought, you know, about that day at the lawyer's office. Ms. Maracle. Do you remember that she gave me an envelope?"

Cass said softly, "You threw it away."

The tears were spilling out of Mom's eyes now, and Cass could feel them as if they were her own. As if they were the tears of lots of people.

"I went out," Mom said. "Down to the bottom of the yard. It was teeming rain. I crossed the little stream and started picking through all that garbage. I know I threw the envelope there. But I couldn't find it. Not anywhere."

She put her head in her hands.

"I ruined everything, didn't I? Story of my life: I'm my own worst enemy. Who knows what was in that envelope? Could have changed our future."

The music stirred inside Cass at that moment. It was a single voice this time. It circled ever higher, just as Cass had done around the white pine in her dream. As it flew higher, it grew bigger.

When Cass spoke, her voice was somehow in harmony with that other voice.

"Mom, the envelope isn't lost."

Mom looked up at her blankly. As if Cass was talking another language altogether.

"I have something to show you," Cass and that other voice said.

Then she was scraping her chair back, and running to her room. She ran to the dresser where the mask had been, and where the envelope now was. She yanked open the drawer and grabbed it. Then she held the envelope to her for a minute.

When she returned to the kitchen, she held it out to Mom.

"See? I rescued it."

Mom took the envelope from Cass with trembling hands. She turned it front to back, and smoothed the paper between her fingers. She began to ease the envelope open.

"Wait!" Cass and the Orenda said.

It was too dark to read. But the overhead lamp would be too bright, too garish for this moment.

Cass took candles from the kitchen drawer and placed them on the table. Mom lit them with matches. The flames made shadows dance on the walls.

It could have been anywhere, any time in history.
It was all times at once.

chapter twenty-four

Mom pulled out the papers and unfolded them. She placed them on the table and slid her hands across the pages to smooth them out. She peered close at the first page and then sat back, putting her hands over it, as if she couldn't quite handle what might be there.

Cass leaned close and put her hand on Mom's.

"Want me to read?"

Mom nodded, closing her eyes.

So Cass hunched over the pages and began to read aloud, in that voice that felt like part herself and part something bigger.

Dear Denise Jane Foster,

I am writing to tell you the story of your
mother. This letter is based on conversations we
had, before she passed away. She helped so many
people during her life, and we, in turn, have tried
to help her by finding you at last.

Mom slid a hand around Cass's shoulders. Her fingers were cold. Cass reached up and took Mom's hand as
if she could thaw it out by holding it.

"Go on," Mom said softly.

Cass leaned close to the page again.

You may have wondered about your own
culture and heritage. You may have felt like you
didn't have any. That is not true. We would like to
give them back to you now.

Your mother was born on the—

Cass's eyes scanned ahead, and she gasped.

"What?" Mom said.

But Cass's heart was beating so fast, suddenly, that
she couldn't answer. And her heart was like drums,
drums that had been waiting for a long time.

Mom gently took the pages.

Your mother was born on the reservation just outside this city. She was Cayuga by birth. You may not know what that means. The Cayuga are one of North America's first nations. They are Iroquois. They have a long and proud history, and you are part of that. We would like you to know that you have roots going back thousands of years in this place.

"Cayuga?" said Mom, trying the word out in her mouth. "Iroquois? So she was…Native?"

The truth was dawning on Cass, falteringly, like she was just learning to walk.

If Mom's mom was Cayuga, then that meant—

It meant—

The drums were pounding joy, and the voices were raised now in victory.

Mom and Cass. They were coming back.

Cass took the pages and began to read again.

Your mother lived on the reservation until she was six years old. Her mother had passed away, and her father raised her as best he could, which was not really very well. The trouble was that he had been forced when he was a little boy to go to a terrible place, where he had forgotten what it was like to have a father, so he couldn't imagine how to be a father. He also tried to find ways to escape his pain, which were not very good ones. That was a very hard thing for everyone.

Then your mother was also taken from her home and sent to one of these nightmare places to live. It was called a residential school. The government said that its purpose was to "take the Indian out of the child." The government and the churches did not think our culture should be part of the country. They tried to get rid of it by taking it away from the children.

Your mother was beaten there, and starved and tormented. Everything was taken away from her, even the words in her mouth. She was punished if she spoke her own language. She learned that her traditions were bad. She learned that if she was to survive, she must be trained to do jobs that would suit her for being a worker in a white society. She must be trained not to be herself.

Cass was dizzy with all the truths that were suddenly all around her. She thought of her dreams of those terrified children, trapped in that place.

Her grandmother had been one of those children. And her great-grandfather.

That was what the mask had been trying to tell her. It was making sure they weren't forgotten. It was passing their stories to Cass.

"The bullies!" Cass said, her hands in fists.

It seemed like the whole world was nothing but bullies and victims, and nobody could escape being one or the other. Not her grandmother, not Mom, not Cass, or Degan or Ellis. Not even the government of her own country. Orenda and Otkon, two forces, and Otkon won, over and over.

She continued to read aloud.

When she was seventeen, they finally set your mother free.

But now she did not know anything about herself. She had forgotten how to speak to her family, because she didn't know her language anymore. She had almost forgotten what a family even was. She did not know how to be a daughter, and she had no idea about what mothers and fathers were supposed to do either. She had learned that white ways were the real ways, that everything else was fake. She had no solid earth under her, and she could barely stand. She was a toddler, staggering in a world that didn't make any sense.

You can see that this was a terrible thing. It separated her from herself, and she was lost for a very long time. She had nothing to tell her what was right, and like her father before her, she discovered a half-world of drinking and drugs that might help her to not think about herself. She did not respect herself. In fact, she hated herself.

During that time, she found out that she was going to have a baby. She was barely out of her teens. She was living on the city streets now, having left the reservation.

Mom shook her head, hand to her mouth. "Poor girl," she said.

The drums pounded louder.

Your mother could not look after a baby, living in alleys and on sidewalks, exposing you to so many dark things. And so, after you were born, she took you to the hospital and placed you in an armchair in the lobby, wrapped in a towel. She didn't leave a note. From there, you were made a ward of the Crown, and you entered a foster home—the first of many for you. We now know about what these places were like for you. We learned, and then we walked them with you in empathy. We have heard you.

"Who's 'we'?" Mom said.

Cass shook her head, puzzled. Maybe it was generations of ancestors, reaching out to recover all those who had been lost. Maybe it was all of those voices who had been singing together inside her, ever since the mask had introduced her to the Orenda. Maybe it was the children in those schools.

Or maybe it was something else, something she couldn't imagine yet.

Your mother was too ashamed to go home, too ashamed to tell anyone what she had done. But when word finally reached her that her father had died, it pierced through the haze she lived in. It shocked her into grieving at last.

She went back to the reservation then. She entered the house she had lived in. Her room had not changed, as if her father had expected her home any day.

She wandered through the house, trying to

feel any sense of connection to it. On the wall in her room, she saw the mask that had always hung there, carved by her grandfather. He was a member of the false face society, and that mask was used in ceremonies for healing.

She took the mask with her.

Cass and Mom stared at each other.

"Your mask?" Mom said.

Your mother was faced with a choice—to continue in her destructive ways, or to seek a means to heal herself. Your mother bravely chose healing. She did not know how to do this, though. So she traveled in search of answers, working as she went to make enough money to continue her quest. She visited other countries and sought out quiet, holy places. She learned to meditate. She studied about great religions, and explored what it felt like to practice them.

When she finally came home, she was ready to look at her own traditions, the spiritual ways of her own people. Humbly, she asked the knowledge keepers to teach her.

And so she began her journey back to herself.

As she learned more and more about herself and her people, she thought more and more about you. She contacted the Children's Aid to ask where you were. They were not helpful, for she had no proof of being your mother. She tried exploring on her own. She followed leads, found possible foster homes where you had been. Each was a dead end, but she continued to search.

At the same time, she went back to school. She earned scholarships to go to college, and from there to university. Eventually, she earned a degree in social work.

Cass said, squeezing Mom's hand: "That's what you're doing! You're going back to school too!"

"Let's not get ahead of ourselves," said Mom. "I haven't even signed up yet. And we aren't made of money."

"But you will."

"Yes, maybe I will," Mom said softly.

Cass read on.

Your mother wanted to help other people who were like herself. Women who had lost the ways of their traditions. Children of those schools, grown up now, lost in the cities. She wanted to help restore them to themselves. She could see that this was to be her job.

So when she was able to, she founded a place for them. It is called the Turtle Island Healing Center. It is in this city.

Cass flung down the papers.

"I know that place! I walked by it with Degan."

Her grandmother had founded it!

Suddenly the amazing truth was dawning on her. The journey she had taken, first in her dream and then with Degan, had been about much more than simply finding the mask. It had been about trying to help her find everything.

Mom took the papers now, and read on.

Your mother made the Turtle Island Healing Center a refuge for all who were hurting. As time went on, she gathered other people to help her. They provided classes in traditional ways, offered aid to those in crisis, helped to build skills necessary for finding jobs. They taught about what it was to be a parent and to be a child.

And during all of this time, the mask hung on the wall of her office.

It reminded her of her own past. It reminded her of her grandfather, and of her father, and of the many children who grew into fathers and mothers without having had any.

You were one of the children she thought of often.

When she became ill, she made a will. In it, she left her house and her little savings to you, even though she did not know where you were.

And then she passed away.

You cannot even begin to imagine the outpouring of grief. We were united in our love for her—those of us who had come, broken, through the open doors, and those of us who had stood by her side and reached out to the ones who thought they were forever lost.

It was a long time before we decided upon a fitting tribute to her. But when we did, it seemed so simple and so obvious.

We must find you.

It was not easy. We knew it wouldn't be. But we were a network of people, not simply one person. Through your mother, we had built roots and connections that spread out in all directions, interlocking and crisscrossing. Although we might have come to the Healing Center broken, we had gone from there to build many kinds of lives. Among us were lawyers, police, and, indeed, social workers within the very Children's Aid itself, who all assisted in our search.

In the end, we found you, of course.

One of us, now a lawyer, met with you and arranged everything. Others cleaned your mother's house and got it ready for you. We put your mother's story into this letter and sealed it.

Finally, we decided to put your mother's mask in the house. We chose not to hang it on the wall, as you did not yet understand its significance. Instead, we placed it quietly in a drawer. It is a sacred thing.

And now you know the main facts. Maybe that's all you will want to know. Or maybe you'll be curious to find out more. Please be assured that we will never seek to contact you or influence you in any way. If you are interested in reaching out to us, however, we will always be here for you.

Cass and Mom sat silently, the letter lying on the table between them.

Mom's eyes were wide in the candlelight, taking in everything, trying to make sense of it.

"She tried to find me," she said at last.

Then her eyes glistened with tears. "And I pawned her mask."

"But if you hadn't," Cass whispered, the drums still beating inside her, "we would never have found out."

Just then, there was a soft knock on the door.

chapter twenty-five

Mom opened the door a little, peering around it into the wet evening. Cass sat at the kitchen table, half-expecting it to be the people who had written the letter.

But instead she heard Degan's low voice.

"Hello, is Cass home?"

Mom opened the door a little wider. "Yes. Please—come in."

She stood aside while Degan stepped into the kitchen. He was sopping wet, water dripping down him and onto the floor. He noticed and stepped backward apologetically. In so doing, he banged into another person behind him.

"No, don't worry about the floor," Mom said. "I'll get you a towel."

So Degan stepped forward again, and the person behind him did too.

It was Ellis, looking like a drowned weasel.

"What are you doing here?" Cass said tightly.

Degan held his hand up. "No, wait. He sneaked out and followed me home, and we've been talking. My aunt said we could come over here. He has something to tell you, and you should listen."

"Why should I?"

She felt as though she was done with bullies, could not tolerate another. And here he was in her own kitchen. In the kitchen of her grandmother, who had suffered bullies too. She did not feel like forgiving just now.

Degan poked Ellis. "Go ahead."

Ellis cleared his throat.

"I bought the mask to—to give it to you. I was trying to figure out a way to do it."

His face flushed brighter pink than usual.

"Why?" Cass said flatly.

Ellis shook his head to get the wet hair out of his eyes, and water sprayed everywhere. "Because you hate me. You called me a bully. I wanted to show you I wasn't."

Cass was opening her mouth to let Ellis know exactly the many ways he was a bully. But Degan raised his hand to hush her.

"Go on and tell her the rest, the way you told me."

Ellis said quietly, "I had it in my desk all day today, but I couldn't get up the nerve to give it to you. I never meant to keep it for myself."

Cass roared, "You had it in your *desk*?"

He couldn't meet her eye. He started playing with one of the toggles on his rain jacket, knotting it into figure eights. "I took it home after school. I was going to try again to give it to you tomorrow. But then you came over, and Dad barged in, and it was bad." He paused. "As—you know."

Then his voice came faster.

"When I heard him talking to you, I heard it. What you were talking about. Those horrible things he said. *He* is a racist! And he's a bully."

Bitterly, he yanked the string of the raincoat.

"He only has respect for one kind of kid. Good at sports, a tough guy, interested in making money one day. Which I'm not. Not any of those things. And my mom wants me to be the best in the class, so she can brag to her stupid friends about all my test results. And I never am best in the class, so I can't please her either."

Now he was knotting the two bottom strings with the toggle on the raincoat pocket, twisting and crumpling the fabric. "I'm just like he says. Only good at making stupid things. Building stuff, and not even useful stuff. Dumb little robots, animals, houses, planes. It's all I want to do, though. I just want to make things."

He glanced over at Degan.

"And you're sketching all the time. I guess—I guess I thought we were kind of the same that way. But turns out I couldn't say it right."

There was a silence as everyone digested this.

"Dirty Indian," Degan said helpfully. "Doesn't want to pay tax. Going to scalp you. No, I'm not sure you said it exactly right."

But there was no bitterness in his voice. As if deep down he had known this about Ellis all along.

Ellis shrugged out of his backpack, placed it on the floor, and unzipped it. He looked up at Cass anxiously.

"Anyway, here it is."

Cass stepped forward, scarcely able to believe what she thought might be inside. With trembling hands, she reached into the backpack. Her fingers met with something soft and matted, masses of it. And there was solid wood, carved into rivulets flowing around a face.

She put loving hands around it, and lifted gently, while the Orenda surged in her, like a mighty singing river.

Mom came in at that moment with a pile of towels. "You must both be freezing. Here, dry off, get your coats off. I was going to make some grilled cheese for me and Cass; we haven't eaten yet. Why don't you stay and have some?"

Mom sounded so confident suddenly, nothing like the mom who was terrified to talk to people. She was different already, different from how she had been before reading the letter, like time was starting to be measured anew after learning the truth about herself. It was like BCE and CE, Otkon and Orenda, the time before and after the letter.

Cass thought back to the stories Mom used to make up for her about being royalty. In a way, the stories had come true. Cass and Mom were part of a line that went back a thousand years. They were not drifting anymore, but had roots binding them to the earth.

Mom started handing towels out. Then she saw the mask. She gave a little cry.

"What? Where did you—?"

She couldn't touch it at first, just gazed on it. Finally, she ran a hand across it, fingertips lingering in the deep wrinkles of the lopsided face. She looked up at Cass wonderingly.

"Ellis bought it for us," Cass said. "That's why it wasn't in the pawnshop anymore."

Ellis shrugged at her. Then he muttered, embarrassed, "Just thirty bucks."

"You bought this mask?" Mom stared at Ellis.

He shrugged again, looking like he didn't know what else to do.

"You are such a good, good kid," Mom said, and embraced him. Ellis stood there awkwardly. He didn't look like he was very used to hugs.

"Not really," Ellis said, his voice muffled by Mom's hug. "I've been—pretty bad, actually."

Mom stood back, and looked him in the eye.

"A bad kid," Mom said, "would not have bought our mask back for us. You are the opposite of a bad kid."

Ellis blushed nearly crimson.

"Maybe he's going to be, anyway," Cass said.

Then Mom rushed around the kitchen, turning on the oven, putting cheese on bread, heating up milk for hot chocolate. Cass, Degan, and Ellis sat at the table, their faces lit by the candles. The light tied them all together, the boys and Cass and Mom, like they were all parts of the same living thing.

And in the center of the table, its curving smile glimmering in the candlelight, lay the mask. Generations of voices sang that it was home at last.

epilogue

That night, Cass dreamed again.

୧

She was standing in the little backyard of her house. The sun was shining overhead, the blue sky dotted with clouds moving quickly on the breeze. Music was all around, in the waving of wildflowers, the rustling of leaves, the beating of birds' wings overhead. Everything all around, inside and out, was bathed in the same song of life, of wildness, although it took many forms. It was as if Cass's mask had become part of everything living and nonliving.

Mom came up beside her and put an arm around her shoulders. Cass slid an arm around Mom's waist. They stood enjoying the great flow of music and light all around.

"Come on," Mom said.

They began to walk together through the yard, and then down the little hill toward the river. Shadows darted across the ground from the waving branches overhead. A million different shades of green and gold tossed all about.

As they descended the hill farther, the colors grew richer and darker, more saturated. Toward the bottom of the hill, Cass could barely see anymore, except for the silhouettes of moving lines—trees arching, branches bending toward each other in an ancient dance. It didn't seem strange to Cass to see the trees dancing. She suddenly felt they had been dancing all along, but she hadn't seen it. Everything, everyone on Earth and maybe in the universe itself, was part of it.

A dark figure moved amid the trees, swaying to the same melody and rhythm. It wove in and out, as if in an elaborate pattern only it knew.

"Who's that?" Cass said.

"I don't know," Mom whispered.

The figure disappeared around one trunk and reappeared in front of another. As it grew nearer, Cass could make out some details. The woman's hair fell around her *face in living strands, each chiming a note that entered and mingled with the great song. Her face was smooth and calm. As she drew ever closer, though, her eyes were not. They sparkled brown, and somehow the sparkles showered thin chimes over the music.*

The lady ran toward them, smiling.

Mom frowned. "Who are you?"

The lady smiled. "Can you guess?"

Mom gazed on the lady's face for a long while, searching and searching. The lady stood and allowed it, making herself very still. It was as if Mom was an animal that was not quite tame, and the lady knew she needed to give Mom all the time in the world to get used to things.

At last Mom gave a little cry, and raised her hands to her mouth.

Then the lady reached out and placed her hands upon Mom's. She drew them away from Mom's face, and clasped them in her own, holding them tight so that she and Mom formed a circle.

And something flowed into Mom's face, something that filled her up inside and made the music all around suddenly charged with a new rhythm and intensity.

The lady turned to Cass.

She let go of one of her hands, so that she and Mom both had a hand free. They held them out to Cass.

Falteringly, Cass stepped forward. She reached out and took each of their hands.

Something nearly electric shot through her. She looked from one to the other, and she knew at last who she saw.

In that moment, her grandmother began to pull upon their hands, and the three began to dance together, spinning slowly at first, and then faster. As they spun, they began to change.

Mom's face lost its tired, tight, worried look and smoothed out. It grew lighter, younger. Her hair was growing, flowing around her shoulders. And Mom was getting smaller.

"Mom!" Cass cried.

Mom laughed aloud. "My darling!"

She was a young girl, just Cass's age.

On the other side, there stood another girl. Her hair hung far down her back. Her face was fearless and glad.

"Come on!" she cried.

They ran together, the three of them.

about the author

SUSAN CURRIE is a winner of Second Story Press' Aboriginal Writing Contest, resulting in this, her second book. Her first book was *Basket of Beethoven*, a finalist for the Silver Birch Award, the Manitoba Young Reader's Choice Award, and the Canadian Library Association Book of the Year for Children. Susan has an MA in children's literature and an ARCT in piano performance from The Royal Conservatory. For the last 17 years, she has been an elementary teacher with the Peel District School Board, for which she received an Award of Distinction. Prior to teaching, she worked as a piano teacher, music director and accompanist. Susan is an adopted person who made contact with a birth aunt a few years ago and subsequently learned about her Cayuga heritage. *The Mask That Sang* grew out of the experience of discovering those roots, and of learning that her grandmother attended residential school. Susan lives in Brampton, Ontario with her family.